THE WHITE W lifted to show the shoulders rose. St Conan.

THE MAN GRIPPED his sword's handle loosely, avoiding tension that would slow him, and began to circle to his right.

THE WOLF TURNED to follow Conan's progress. The rumble increased. Conan watched as it gathered itself for a spring.

THE WOLF LEAPED, aiming for Conan's throat. Lithely, the Cimmerian youth bounded to one side, out of the creature's path. He swung the big broadsword around and over his head, as might a man splitting wood with an axe, but kept his shoulders down, as he had been taught.

THE WOLF'S SPEED was deceptive. Conan's swing, had it connected with the beast's neck or body, would have dealt it a killing blow. As it happened, the razored edge of the sword met instead the tip of the beast's tail, and severed it neatly.

THE WOLF HOWLED and spun, but its balance was altered by the missing segment of tail. Having adjusted for his earlier error, Conan's second cut was more accurate. His blade sang in the frosty air, a cold melody of iron and blood, and the edge of the sword met the gristle and bone of the dire-wolf's neck. The contest went to the man and forged metal.

But the Men With No Eyes were harder to defeat....

Look for all these Conan books from Tor

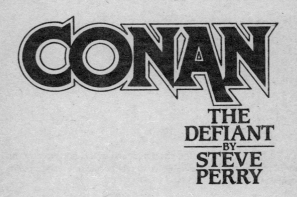

CONAN

THE DEFIANT
BY
STEVE PERRY

A TOM DOHERTY ASSOCIATES BOOK

CONAN THE DEFIANT

Copyright © 1987 by Conan Properties, Inc.

A TOR Book
Published by Tom Doherty Associates, Inc.
49 West 24 Street
New York, NY 10010

Cover art by Sean Joyce

ISBN: 0-812-54273-8   Can. ISBN: 0-812-54274-6

First edition: October 1987
First Mass Market edition: August 1988

Printed in the United States of America

0 9 8 7 6 5 4 3 2 1

For Dianne, and love constantly changing;
For Dal and Steph, nearly grown;
And for Jon and Jess, still a way to go

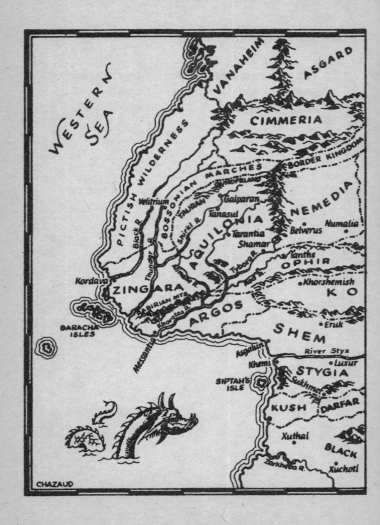

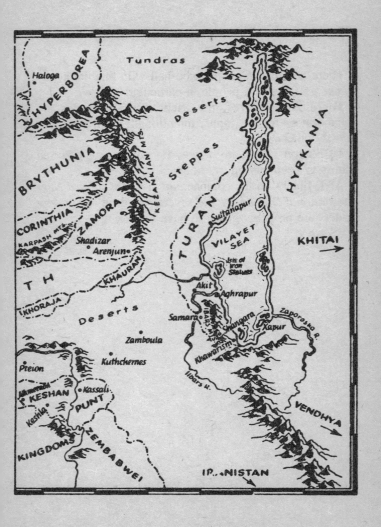

There are always people who help. On this book, my thanks go to several people in particular:

To Michael Reaves, my friend and sometimes my collaborator, for his input, intentionally and otherwise (mostly otherwise);

To Sharon Jarvis, my agent, for convincing assorted editors to keep buying my books;

And, finally, to the compilers of *Webster's Third New International Dictionary,* for several words at least a few readers are probably going to have to look up.

SCP

Prologue

Neg the Malefic walked in the chambers of the dead.

It was only fitting that he travel such musty and dank places, for he was a necromancer, and his power oozed like dark syrup from those no longer among the living. More than a worker of simple death-spells, Neg kept captives in the cold chambers beneath the malignant temple peopled by the Men With No Eyes. Men called Neg's ensorcelled the dead-not-dead, or called them zombies, and made signs to ward off evil when they spoke of such things. The necromancer laughed at the thought. Men were sheep, and Neg was a shepherd. Someday, he would rule the living as he now ruled his undead.

Shadows danced on the soot-stained walls, flickering patterns cast by the black tapers guttering in their tarnished green brass holders. Smoke fled from the small flames to further paint darkness upon the walls and ceiling, to stir the spiders in their webs. No living man ventured here by choice; even the Men With No Eyes came only to tend the candles, and that only at Neg's command. They had no need of light, and the zombies at Neg's beck no longer cared to see one another. The undead were held in thrall, and wished nothing more than to slip the magical tether holding them from the Gray Lands.

Neg laughed, and the sound echoed along the deserted corridor, bouncing from the rock walls and back upon itself. No doubt his undead wished to leave his hospitable embrace. Alas, he could not allow that, for they had too much to give to depart with it. They had traveled across the River of Death, and been forced to return. They knew things normal living men did not know. And through them, Neg also learned these secrets. Such knowledge was power in the hands of one so skilled as he had become over the years.

An umber rat chittered at him as the magician passed, disturbed in its meal upon what appeared to be a human finger bone. Neg fixed the rodent with his baleful stare, and the rat fell silent, struck by the power of the killing gaze. The rat shivered, emitted one final squeak, and collapsed. Its naked pink tail twitched nervously as it died.

Neg smiled.

He passed from the dank hallway into a massive chamber. Thick black mold graced the walls in mottled patches, and the flickering light did little to keep the darkness at bay. The reek of death was stronger here, holding sway in the must-laden air. The click of Neg's boots against the grimy flagstones echoed hollowly in the vast room.

Neg strode to the center of the room, unaffected by the dark, a man certain of his path. He took a deep breath, drinking in the odor of decay as an ordinary mortal might inhale the aroma of a fine perfume. His realm. His.

"Come," he commanded. His voice danced against the distant walls and bounced back at him, hollow, as had been his footsteps.

The darkness stirred. There came the creak of sinew, the rustle of tomb-dried clothing, the shuffle of rotten leather against stone. The hard chill that wrapped Neg seemed to increase, driving icy talons deeper into his body, into his very essence. That, too, was a part of his strength. A slight breeze arose, stirring Neg's long hair. Once, his hair had been black, so black it had seemed blue; but gray had long since taken command of the magician's locks. It had been five hundred years since he had seen the visage of a young man in his glass. But no matter; he had also long since ceased to age as did ordinary men.

The unseen things in the chamber drew closer, forming a circle around Neg with their sounds. Closer, yet closer—

"Hold!"

All sound ceased. No breath save Neg's own disturbed the stillness of the room.

"Who am I?" Neg called.

Thirty voices spoke as one. "Master," they said. But the sound was hushed, the intonation flat, the spirit dull.

"Aye, Master I am and shall remain, until I deem it otherwise. Never forget it." He paused, to enjoy his control. Silence surrounded him as might a blanket of dark wool. He spoke again. "Who knows of the Source of Light?"

"I know," came a deep male voice.

"Come closer."

The shuffle of feet on stone sounded.

Neg snapped his fingers, the click sounding like the breaking of a dry stick, or, perhaps, a dried bone. A small flame erupted from the blackened nail of his thumb, and yellow light fought the gloom, penetrating but a small distance. It was enough of a lamp to reveal the gray and expressionless features of a dead man.

"Hold. Speak. Why has it not been delivered to me?"

The man's lips moved, but he stared straight ahead, as if looking into some far land. "Vultures pick at the corpses of your agents in the shadow of the Great Wall of Koth."

"By Set's Black Hand! What happened? Speak quickly!"

The dull voice droned on. "Your men slew the Khauranian tribesman and obtained the talisman as you ordered. But they sought to increase the weight of their purses by selling the stolen fetish to a mage in the Kothian city of Khalis. Instead of gold, the mage would have paid them with the poisonous essence of black lotus. A struggle ensued. Your men died."

"Fools! I shall call them back from Gehanna and make them beg for death for a thousand years!" Neg spat upon the flagstones, his rage riding high, tightening his thin shoulders. Those men would suffer, indeed, but—what of the talisman? He voiced his question.

"In the struggle, the magician was also slain," the zombie said. "The Source of Light fell into the grasp of a priest. The device even travels toward the Temple of the Suddah Oblates."

"*No!*"

"Yes." What seemed a faint smile flitted across the face of the dead man.

Neg snatched at his purse, digging out a handful of coarse translucent-white crystals. He flung this at the zombie, and the shower of material followed the path of the whuffing flame surrounding the magician's thumb. The zombie emitted a low moan as the crystals touched his face. From each contact with the crystals came a sizzling sound, as fat dropped into a cookfire sputters, and smoke boiled forth from the burning flesh. The zombie collapsed in a boneless fashion, released from the life-giving spell by the magicked salt Neg threw at him.

The necromancer glared down at the corpse. "Nay, you shall not escape that easily. Enjoy your brief moment in the Gray Lands, my thrall, for I shall snatch you back to serve me again soon enough!"

The small fire on his hand vanished as Neg glared at it, and the magician spun and started for the chamber's exit. "Out of my way! Go back to your slumber and its nightmares!"

As the mage stalked angrily from the chamber, the enthralled zombies began their tired shambling back to the edges of their prison. Upon the floor, the magicked salt hissed and evaporated in a greasy yellow cloud, filling the air with the taint of burned sulphur and brimstone. The zombies looked longingly at the vanishing salt. It had carried release for one of their number; all of them knew that the touch of Neg's magic was the only hope for their own freedom. But the salt was gone, and with it, their hope.

In the darkness, unmoving, stood a woman known as Tuanne. She had been beautiful in life, and in death had kept her beauty, due to the whim of Neg the Malefic. She alone stood unmoving, disobeying the necromancer's command. A single crystal of the magical salt had flown past its intended target to land upon her full and shapely breast. The thin silk of her dress was unaffected, but the salt had burned that tender breast, as a hot needle would burn. The pain was intense, but she did not cry out.

For, along with the pain, Tuane realized that the spell holding her enthralled was no longer in force.

The others reached their destination and fell once again into nightmarish slumber, but Tuanne stood fixed, full of questions. Was this some cruel trick of Neg's? If she tried to leave the chamber, would he be waiting? How could this have happened? The touch of enspelled brack had always returned the zombies to death before. Could it be that such a small amount merely destroyed part of the spell? Was she truly free?

No, Tuanne decided, she was not free. Whatever else might be, she was still a zombie, not dead and not really alive. She had been held in this state by the evil wizard for a hundred years. All those she had known in life now walked the Gray Lands. She had been denied her rightful place among them, and she wished for nothing as much as that rightful place, as did all the other zombies Neg held.

Well. If it were not a trick, if she truly had slipped the noose by which she had been tethered, what could she do now? Neg held the key to her death, and he would have but to look at her to restore his control again. There must be something she could do, however, to break completely free of this ensorcelled state. And there must be some way to help the others Neg held captive.

Tuanne searched her memories, both in life and in her brief walks across the Gray Lands. After a moment, the answer swam up through the depths of her mind, a clear and shining light in the murk: that was the solution. Light. The Source of Light which Neg sought to increase his powers. That talisman held her release, along with the release of the others in this hellish chamber. She must find the fetish and use it to free herself and the others. Yes. That was what she would do.

The beautiful zombie slowly walked to the exit, smiling for the first time in a hundred years. She would do whatever she must to obtain the Source of Light.

Whatever she had to do. . . .

One

The young man came from the north, through the mountains, the cold and jagged teeth that separate Hyperborea from Brythunia. His name was Conan, and he was well-muscled and tall beneath the crusty furs he wore. He carried a heavy broadsword of ancient blued iron, still sharp but notched from battles long past. He had taken the blade from across the thigh bones of a corpse, and very nearly died for his trouble. He shivered at the memory. It had been unnatural, that moldering corpse, and he had no love for such dark magics. A man who trucked with such things could lose his soul.

An icy wind ruffled Conan's black mane, but the cold fire of his blue eyes was untroubled by the weather. In Cimmeria, the land of his birth, such winds were a part of life, to be accepted as one of Crom's small tests.

He had been walking for several days, living on roots and late-season berries, and a few snared rabbits. It was a hard trek, but better than the time before. Anything was better than slavery, even the wolves who had pursued

7

him for two days after his escape. The wolves were gone, and should they return, he now had the sword.

Conan's keen gaze searched the rocks along his path. He had been looking for a particular kind, and finally, he saw it. A whetstone to repair the notches in his blade. It was a lesson he had learned well from his father: Always keep your steel sharp and smooth; a rough edge lends itself to weakness and breakage.

An hour with the stone gave the sword a new sheen and sharpness, and even the deepest nicks were reduced to smooth steel. He swung the weapon back and forth and grinned. As the son of a smith, he had a practical familiarity with bronze and iron, and this blade was superb, in balance and in temper.

Taking the sword had given the young Cimmerian the glimmer of an idea. The corpse, for all its activity after the blade had been removed from its skeletal embrace, had no further use for the weapon, while Conan certainly had. There existed many rich men who had much more gold than they could ever use; therefore, taking a portion of it here and there would hardly inconvenience them. There was, Conan had heard, a city to the south, in Zamora, where many rich merchants lived, along with their stores of treasure. A thief might do well for himself there, and Conan meant to travel to the city, called Shadizar, and test the theory.

How far it was to Shadizar, the Cimmerian did not know. He would travel south until he found it. Since leaving the mysterious crypt he had fallen into while pursued by the wolves, Conan had not set gaze upon another human being. He had seen rabbits, bears, and even a great cat prowling the mountains; unfortunately, he was not apt to get directions from beasts. He smiled at the thought.

A scream broke into the young man's smile, and he leaped to his feet, the sword held ready to strike.

The sound echoed from down the mountain, in the direction he intended to travel. He was curious, but not foolish. His capture into slavery had not lessened his bravery; however, it had taught him caution. One who always leaped without first looking was an imbecile, and Conan of Cimmeria was no man's fool. He moved toward the sound quickly but cautiously, alert for signs of danger.

At first glance, it appeared that a single swordsman stood against five antagonists, themselves armed with swords, long dirks, and spears. The single man, dressed in a dark robe, had his back protected by the steep slope of the mountain and faced the others across a short stretch of rocky ground, angled slightly downward. The robed figure was outnumbered, certainly, but he had the high ground and the others could not get behind him.

Conan's first thought was to leap into the fray, and he nearly did so, on the side of the single man, simply because of the odds. He held back at the last instant. Perhaps it was better to watch a moment and see what transpired. The big Cimmerian did move closer, still unseen by the combatants.

One of the five darted in, swinging his curved sword downward at the head of the robed man. The defender leaped to his left and brought his own weapon down in an angular slash, catching the curved-sword wielder on the right ribs.

There came a sound like a ripe melon dropped upon flagstones.

Conan blinked, surprised. It was no sword the robed man held, but a short wooden stick, a slightly curved cane of sorts.

The attacker groaned and fell back, tripping over one of his comrades and dropping his blade to clutch at his battered torso.

A second attacker thrust a spear at the robed man's side, and Conan was surprised again, at the speed of the parry. The robed figure spun tightly and cut downward with the cane, blocking the spear. He continued the circular motion upward, shoved the spear away, then followed through with a crack upon the spearman's shoulder. Conan heard the wet snap of bone.

The third attacker managed to get his spear between the legs of the cane fighter then, and tripped him. The fourth and fifth men moved in for the kill.

Conan yelled to distract the attackers, and leaped at them, his newly sharpened blade whistling as he swung it back and forth. What they thought of this fur-covered apparition he did not know, but the men gave ground.

The spearman who had tripped the cane fighter thrust his weapon's point at Conan's breast, and the young Cimmerian chopped the wooden shaft in half with a single stroke.

A large man slashed at Conan with a wicked-looking dirk, tearing a gaping hole in his furs and raising a bloody furrow over Conan's hip. Enraged, Conan turned and swung his blade. The sharp iron sang, then tore a path through the man's face at the eyes, slinging the resulting gore across his nearest companion. The cut man was dead where he stood, and his soul fled before he finished his fall to the stony ground.

In a moment the cane fighter was up, and seeing that the odds were so changed, the remaining men fled, leaving the dead one behind.

Conan stood watching them run, breathing great clouds

of vapor into the cool air. Next to him the robed man stood tall in a ready position, the tip of his cane held at throat-level, also watching the attackers flee. After a moment he thrust the cane under his belt and bent to examine the fallen man.

"Dead," he pronounced. Conan thought he heard a tinge of regret in the man's deep voice.

"Aye," the Cimmerian said. "I hope I chose the right side."

"Such would depend upon one's viewpoint," the man said. "From mine, you certainly chose well." He glanced down at the fallen man. "From his, I cannot say, but I suspect he would be most unhappy." The man held his hands out, to show that both were empty. "I am called Cengh, a poor priest of the Suddah Oblates." He was a tall man, though not so tall as Conan, with light hair and a short beard. He was perhaps thirty years old.

"I am Conan, of Cimmeria, late of Hyperborea."

"Well met, Conan. Tell me, what prompted you to join my side instead of that of the assassins?"

"Five against one seemed unfair." Conan pointed at the cane through Cengh's belt. "Had you a real blade, you might have killed them and won the fight on your own."

"We do not hold with killing men," Cengh said. "Even mountain bandits who have no such scruples."

"But you have nothing against breaking their bones."

"Ah, no."

Conan shrugged. His business finished, he turned to depart.

"But wait," Cengh called. "Where are you going?"

"I travel to Zamora."

"You have saved my life. You must allow me to repay you."

"You could tell me if I am on the right track to Shadizar."

"A wicked place," Cengh said. "Full of thieves and trulls. Why would you wish to go there?"

Conan grinned. "A business opportunity."

"But you are wounded." He pointed at the cut on Conan's hip.

"A scratch. It will heal."

"Shadizar is a month's journey from here on foot. I travel to the Temple That Will Not Fall, the center of the Suddah Oblates, only two days from here. Come with me, so that we may extend our hospitality and replace your clothes, if nothing else."

Conan's first inclination was to refuse. He wanted nothing to do with priests or temples; still, the stinking furs he wore were about to rot away. And, the idea of a hot meal and a sheltered bed for a few days was not repulsive. He had saved the man's life, after all, and in his position, Conan would certainly wish to offer some means of repayment. A man paid his debts. It was only fitting that he give the priest a way to offer his gratitude.

"Aye. I suppose a few days delay would not be amiss."

The region in which they traveled continued rocky and mountainous. Cengh told Conan that the Kenzankian Range ran the entire way along the eastern borders of Brythunia and Zamora, to Khauran. Once across the high hills between Hyperborea and Brythunia, there was a north-south road which was more than a little easier to tread than the snowy wastes.

Conan was curious about Cengh's use of the cane, and expressed it so.

The priest smiled. "Ah, while we oppose violence, there are, unfortunately, times when nothing else will

suffice. Wild beasts seldom listen to reason, and there are
some men who seem little better than animals. Our found-
ers, being a pragmatic lot, decided to devise some forms
of protection. Thus, we have weapons—canes, staves,
certain kinds of nets, ropes—but we try to avoid using
even those.''

The path rose steeply, and Conan found himself occupied with his footing upon the ice-slicked rocks. ''How
then,'' he said, after reaching a fairly level area, ''do you
take game?''

''We do not. We eat no meat or fowl. Nothing with
warm blood. We do consume fish.''

Conan shook his head, but did not speak. No meat?
How did a man keep his blood red without meat? Of
course, he had not eaten much of that himself of late, but
that was through no lack of desire. Then again, Cengh
seemed no less of a man than many Conan had met in his
young life. Certainly at least two of the brigands who had
attacked him had reason to know as much.

''In any event,'' Cengh said, ''I am but a novice with
the *fimbo*.'' He patted the curved cane. ''At The Temple
That Will Not Fall, Oblate Kensash, who wears sixty-five
winters and hair as white as hoarfrost, demonstrates *real*
proficiency.''

Conan nodded. As a warrior, he looked forward to seeing
that.

The pair still had a day's journey ahead of them when
the Temple That Would Not Fall came into view. Conan
immediately saw how the place came to be so named: it
was a massive stone structure perched impossibly on a thin
spire of rock. It seemed to Conan nothing so much as a
plate heaped with mounds of fruit, balanced on a straw.

He felt a chill as he stared at the temple. Surely no natural structure could exist in such a manner. And to the young Cimmerian, anything unnatural was linked with magic, as surely as ancient Atlantis had been swallowed by the oceans.

Cengh smiled at the vision, and Conan held his own face in an expressionless mask. He would not reveal fear to this man.

The path became steeper, ceasing to be a walk for a climb at stretches. Climbing presented no obstacle to a Cimmerian, however, and Cengh even made to remark upon Conan's prowess.

"In Cimmeria we send children to gather firewood on steeper slopes," Conan said. That was not strictly true, since few parents had children to spare to the falling death, but often children would ascend rocky spires on their own. He had done so often enough as a boy.

As the pair began walking a flatter stretch of ground, Cengh stopped suddenly, as if listening.

Conan strained his own ears, searching for any unusual sound. Just ahead stood a snow-shrouded jumble of large boulders, with scraggly, dark green bushes obscuring the bases of several of the rocks. The path then wound off to the left, and seemed to change into a series of hand- and footholds as it ascended once again. He listened, and there came to him only the wind, moaning across rocky hollows; a distant bird *crawed*; nothing else—wait. There was something. A kind of high-pitched rattle. He had heard something similar before—a serpent he had seen in the desert, winding sideways across the evening sands. It, too, had made a sound much like this one. When the snake had made for Conan, he had flattened its head with a stone and discovered the source of the noise: a series of horny chambers on the snake's tail, containing tiny beads.

"Is it a serpent?" Conan asked.

"Worse." He drew his cane and straightened.

In a moment, Conan saw what the priest meant.

From behind the largest of the boulders emerged something unlike anything Conan had ever seen. Tall it was, at least his own height, and it had two arms and two legs. This beast, however, had never seen the inside of a human womb. It was some form of reptile, scaled and grayish-green, and it dragged a tail as thick as Conan's thigh where it joined the body, tapering to a point thinner than a man's fingertip. It had the face of a lizard, slits for nostrils, and yellow eyes, with fleshy, oddly puckered lips. It looked as if it meant to whistle with those lips. On top of its bony head was the compartmented plate that rattled as it moved, much as the thing had been on the serpent's tail. It had short arms, with three claws on each. It seemed to smile, and in so doing, revealed pointed teeth the size and shape of a child's dagger.

"It's a stith," Cengh said, answering Conan's unasked question. "Do not allow it to spit on you."

Conan unlimbered his sword, never taking his gaze from the stith. "Will it attack an armed man?"

"Aye. It will attack fifty armed men. And kill more than it can eat, for sport. A hellish beast."

"How fast is it?"

The stith's smile faded and it pursed its lips again.

"Too fast to run from," Cengh said.

The stith shuffled toward the two men, lashing its tail back and forth, catlike.

Conan took a tighter grip upon the stained leather handle of his sword. "To the left," he ordered. "I will take the right."

But before the two could move, the stith gathered itself

and sprang, bounding toward Conan in great hops, like a rabbit, using its fat tail for balance.

Fast it was, and no mistake about that! Conan leaped to his right and raised his sword, just as the stith spat a stinking stream of glowing emerald liquid at where the man had just been. The effulgent lance spattered upon the rocky ground, and the expectoration raised dank smoke where it touched.

"Crom!" Conan swung his sword, chopping downward as the stith bounded past, but his reaction to the acidic sputum slowed his reflexes. Instead of bisecting the stith's head, he merely hacked off the tip of its tail.

The stith was unhappy with the action. It screamed, a sound like a child touching a hot kettle, and spun, spraying another line of vivid green at its tormentor.

Conan dodged, twisting so the brilliant stream passed his shoulder and chest by less than a thumb's thickness. He shuffled backward, cocking his blade by his ear.

The stith turned and inhaled deeply, prepared to spit again, Conan did not doubt.

"Hai!"

Cengh's yell was followed by the *thwack!* of his cane across the spine of the stith.

The monster coughed, and blew a mist of somewhat duller green instead of the thin jet. Conan felt a stinging on his face and bare arms, but he twirled away from the malignant fog and recocked his blade over his shoulder.

The stith spun toward Cengh and inhaled sharply.

Conan leaped and swung his sword in a flat horizontal arc. The newly sharped edge sliced through the scaled neck, slowed briefly as it passed between two vertebrae, and exited opposite the point of its entry. Blood gouted and fountained as the stith's head tumbled from its body and smacked into the hard ground. The quivering, headless body leaped once, reflexively, then fell.

The young Cimmerian stared at the dead beast in wonder. If the priests knew these things stalked the mountain crags and yet went armed only with sticks, they were either brave men or fools. Perhaps both.

Two

"**S**now!" Cengh yelled.

Conan stared at the priest. Had the man taken leave of his senses?

"Get to the snow, over by the rocks," Cengh commanded. "Quickly."

At first Conan thought perhaps the stith had a mate; or mayhaps the beasts somehow feared snow, but that thought was erased after a moment. When the two men reached the crusty summer snow maintained by the shadows of the boulders, the priest gathered up a double handful and made as if to shove it into Conan's face. The young Cimmerian took a step backward, bringing his gore-smeared blade up. "What foolishness is this?"

"The stith's poison," Cengh said. "We must wash it from your skin. Even a small dose brings illness or death."

The younger man recalled the stinging he had felt when the now-dead beast had coughed at him. Ah. He put his sword on the ground and scooped at the cold whiteness surrounding his ankles. He scrubbed at his face, feeling the blood rush to his cheeks as the crystals abraded his skin.

After three such applications, Cengh seemed satisfied. But he pointed to a smoking patch on the furs Conan wore near his shoulder. "It will eat through to the skin," the priest said. "Best you remove that portion."

Conan reached for his sword, but Cengh produced a short, curved knife shaped much like a tooth. "Here, use this."

The Cimmerian took the knife, tested the edge with his thumb, and nodded. The priest kept his blade shaving-sharp. It was but the work of a moment to excise the tainted section of fur.

Cengh then examined Conan's face carefully. "It should serve," he pronounced. "A concentrated splash of the venom is nearly always fatal, but it appears you were dusted only lightly."

Conan used a portion of the contaminated fur just re-moved from his clothing to wipe the blood from his sword. He also returned the curved knife to Cengh. "No rules against knives in your order, eh?"

Cengh grinned as the knife vanished beneath his robe. "Roots must be sliced and fruit sometimes peeled."

Conan did not return the grin. These Oblates might be peaceful, but they were also apt to be dangerous to anyone foolish enough to presume too much on that peacefulness.

"Are there apt to be any more like that one?" Conan waved toward the dead stith.

"Likely not. They are solitary and territorial."

"Considering the terrain, the bandits, and creatures, I suspect your order is not bothered overmuch by visitors," Conan said dryly.

"Very true," Cengh said, just as dryly.

*   *   *

On closer examination, the Temple That Will Not Fall seemed much less magical than Conan had first thought. The rock spire upon which the main bulk of buildings balanced was much thicker than it had seemed at a distance; more, this close the young barbar could see that support struts extended from the spire to the base of the manmade structures. And the struts bore a number of arches, a form that Conan knew added strength. So, perhaps it was clever construction and not magic which kept the temple perched on the rock, though the latter could not be totally discounted. The place was huge, easily the size of a small town or large village.

The priest and the Cimmerian wound up a set of narrow steps cut into the mountain's rock. Ahead loomed a split wooden gate set into a mortared rock wall; both gate and wall were easily thrice the height of a tall man.

Standing outside the gate, Cengh hailed the watch.

"Ho, will the temple allow one of its children entrance?"

A hooded face appeared over the top of the wall and peered down at the two men. "Which child might that be?" the man called back.

"Cengh the Messenger," Conan's companion returned. He pushed his cowl back, revealing his face.

"Ho, Cengh! Welcome! And who might this fur-clad giant with you be?"

"He is Conan of Cimmeria, to whom I owe my life."

"Ah, welcome to you as well, Conan of far Cimmeria."

The man vanished, and in a moment, half of the gate swung inward. The wood was as thick as Conan's chest, and with the movement came the creaks of heavy iron hinges. The rich smells of people, animals, and cooking flowed out with the temple air. The young Cimmerian took in the scents, realizing how long it had been since he had been in civilization.

If anything, the temple was larger than it seemed from without. There were streets, houses, larger buildings, indeed, it should be called the City That Will Not Fall, Conan thought.

Cengh waved at robed figures as he passed them, and they smiled and waved in return. It did not take Conan long to realize that all the people he saw were male. There were children playing here and there, but all boys. He remarked upon this to Cengh.

"True," the priest said. "Women are not allowed inside the temple. We are a celibate order."

Conan considered this for a moment.

"How then do you produce children?"

Cengh laughed. "We do not. Our acolytes journey from all over to join us here."

"Why?"

"It is a good life, especially for the children of poor men. We offer food, shelter, clothing, faith, and knowledge."

"But no women."

"The life of a priest is not for every man."

"Indeed," Conan said. Although young, the Cimmerian knew that much about himself. Eating roots and being without the company of women held no attraction for him.

As the two passed a knot of men examining a basket of fruit, Conan caught a glimpse of a particularly smooth face under one of the cowls. At least one of these young would-be priests looked almost girlish.

Not a few of the robed figures returned Conan's appraising looks. Conan felt his anger bubble as some of the younger boys smiled and pointed at his ragged furs. How many of them had escaped slavery and fought wolves and a corpse? he wondered.

"Pay them no mind, Conan," Cengh said. "They are ignorant of a man's worth. They will learn."

"If they survive." Conan's voice was a low rumble.

A bleating goat ran past, and a fat, robed figure chased it, yelling, "Halt, beast! I have already lost your sister and her milk! Come back!"

Conan laughed at the sight, and his anger, quick to rise, fled just as quickly.

Cengh led Conan to a building cut and assembled from a smooth, white rock. Inside was a pool set into the floor. Warm vapor arose from the surface of the clear water; a clean, sharp scent reached the younger man's nostrils.

"The waters are for soaking," the priest said. "Perhaps you would care to bathe?"

The young Cimmerian giant nodded. Heated water, and clean? Aye, he would care to wash the stench of travel and furs from his muscular form.

"I shall have clothing brought to you. I must go and deliver my message before I can partake of the mint pool myself."

Conan nodded, already stripping the furs from his body. He laid his sword near the edge of the pool and stepped into the water. Ah, here was a pleasure! The water was so hot it raised gooseflesh. Conan sat, and the relaxing hotness rose to his chin. He closed his eyes. Ah . . .

As Cengh made his way toward the Highest Oblate's chambers, he was unaware that one of the ubiquitous robed figures took a special notice of his passage. The figure seemed no different from any of the others attending to various chores along the main thoroughfare of the temple city; it was, however, a counterfeit. The gray robes covered one called Skeer, and he had been many things: thief, footpad, spy, and assassin, but never a priest. His presence inside the Temple That Will Not Fall was the result of careful planning backed by the forces of evil magic.

Skeer drew his pay from Neg, master of necromancy.

Quickly, Skeer established his secretive watch. He was most adept at this, a skill born of long practice, and aided muchly by his appearance. Neg's agent had a face that practically radiated truth and innocence. It had been said of Skeer that should he be caught stabbing a fat merchant repeatedly, he could claim to be merely cleaning his dagger and be believed, such was his countenance.

The priest presented no challenge to his follower's talents. Skeer paused now and then, and pretended to examine his sandal or something of interest in a shop window, but these subterfuges were more to keep in practice than for actual need. Cengh never looked in his shadower's direction. The fool.

Cengh entered a building, and Skeer hurried to follow him. The priest would be delivering a message shortly to someone—Neg's agent did not know to whom—but it was paramount that he be in a position to overhear that message. According to his sources, vital information would be contained in Cengh's recital. Failure to obtain that information would delay Skeer's success in his mission. Neg would not be pleased at any delay, and Skeer most assuredly did not wish to incur the necromancer's displeasure.

He shuddered at the thought.

So it happened that when Cengh delivered himself of a

most important message to the Highest Oblate, a set of
ears for which it had been unintended also received the
words. And a smile came to the lips of a face so angelic
even the mother of its owner's most cruelly murdered
victim would have difficulty disliking it.

Behind a stall for housing rams, Skeer raised a short,
fat-bladed dagger over the breast of a securely trussed
goat. The fat priest would never find his lost beast. Or if
so, it would be in no condition to produce additional milk.
The goat had a greater destiny.

Skeer plunged the dagger downward, and skewered the
animal's heart. Blood pumped, and the man cupped his
hands to catch the warm fluid. He raised his hands and
lowered them thrice, according to the spell, and chanted
the phrase Neg had carefully drilled into him.

> By warmth growing cold,
> by life made dead,
> by the Gray Beyond,
> I seek the Connection!

Skeer then tossed the blood into the air, and drew the
arcane symbol representing Neg upon his left wrist with
blood on the tip of his right forefinger. The air in front of
him shimmered and seemed to thicken. The man shivered.
He had done this several times before, and each time was
no better than the last. He grew cold, as if dipped into a
stream of melted snow.

"SPEAK." The voice came from the rippling air in
front of Skeer, disembodied, but loud and powerful.

"I have the arrival details of that which you seek, lord."

"I EXPECTED NO LESS. WHEN?"

"Three days, lord."

"GOOD. DO NOT FAIL ME, SKEER."

"Never, my lord."

The air shivered, much as the man who beheld it, and all of a moment, returned to its natural state. Skeer took a deep breath, and allowed it to escape slowly. The idea of failure flitted only briefly across his mind. He put the thought away in haste. Best not to think of that.

One of the Men With No Eyes glided to a stop in front of Neg. The necromancer regarded the visage. The name was not accurate, strictly speaking. His servants *did* have eyes. Those globes were entirely white, with what seemed to be clouds shifting back and forth in the milky orbs, so that an ordinary man watching might fear for his sanity. And such optics were useless for seeing, of course. But then, there were certain compensations for blindness.

Neg smiled. To the figure, he said, "Prepare the Chamber. Within a moon, I shall have that which I need to energize it."

The Man With No Eyes nodded once, bowed, and moved smoothly from Neg's personal chamber.

Ah, yes, Neg thought. Skeer had all the cunning of a weasel, and the morality and loyalty, too, but he would do as he was instructed. He feared to do otherwise, and with good reason. Soon. Soon.

A boy brought clothing to the enclosed pool in which Conan soaked. Decent clothing, too, the Cimmerian noted. For a time he had mused that he might be offered a priest's robes, but no, these items were ordinary, save for their good quality. There were underbreeks of some silken cloth, short leathern breeches, thickly cut sandals with long leg ties, a supple leather tunic, and even a belt and purse. The last was quite empty, Conan noted. All this was set upon a thick towel.

Conan stepped from the bath and dried himself, then proceeded to dress. By Crom, the clothing even fit!

As he was lacing the final strap on his new sandal, Cengh returned. He nodded at the Cimmerian, then shucked his robes and sank into the heated and scented waters.

"Ah. The gods be praised for hot water!"

Conan nodded. He felt a great deal better himself.

Cengh said, "If you can spare me a few moments to cleanse away my travel dust, I suspect I can find someone willing to feed us."

The young Cimmerian nodded again. Food would be welcome enough. "Do the Oblates believe in drinking the products of the grape?"

The priest laughed. "Wine? But of course! We are not barbarians—" Cengh fell silent suddenly. "I meant no insult, Conan."

"It is no insult. And barbarians invented wine."

"But priests have become the experts at drinking it," Cengh said. "I shall show you."

The temple of the Men With No Eyes squatted on a dark hillside near the juncture of Corinthia, Brythunia, and Zamora. The forest at the base of the hill was dank, prey to rain that somehow fell harder and more often than it did on the surrounding territory. The storms were often charged with powerful lightning, and raged at the earth with hail and discharges, as well as pounding rains.

It was through this dark forest and in the midst of a driving storm that Tuanne made her escape from Neg the Malefic's domination. Though not living in the way of mortal men, Tuanne had no special powers that allowed her to ignore the mud-slicked ground or the bone-chilling sheets hurled by the storm. Lightning flashed and was chased by its loud brother thunder as the beautiful zombie slipped and slid away from her former prison. Her long, jet hair lay plastered to her head and back, and her flimsy clothing gaped where it had been rent in a dozen places by thorn brambles and untimely falls. More than anything, the normal coldness she felt was intensified, so that her limbs, her breasts, and her cheeks felt as if they had been carved from ice. Those foolish men who thought that zombies felt no pain knew nothing of it.

Tuanne did not know where she was going. All she knew was that the talisman she sought called to her, tugged at her as if it were attached by an invisible string. If she turned away from it, the pull increased. The Source of Light, and her salvation, lay *that* way, to the north and east; therefore, it was that way she would travel. Until she came to the place where the device rested, she herself would not rest. She would obtain the talisman, she would somehow use it to free herself and her brothers and sisters still held by the necromancer. Somehow.

Lightning shattered the darkness, and a nearby fir tree exploded in a spray of wood and sap. Thunder tried to hide the damage, battering at the night. Tuanne started at the light and sound, so close they came almost as one. She fell yet again, and her sodden dress tore, revealing more of her ivory skin to the storm's attack. It did not matter. She would find new clothing. It would not warm her, but that did not matter, either. She had a goal, and a hundred years of wanting it. She would endure until she reached it.

Three

Conan followed Cengh into a large hall filled with robed Oblates. Everyone, save the big Cimmerian, was dressed in the same manner, even the servers. The bath and new clothing suited the young barbar well enough, but the idea of dining on roots and berries created less enthusiasm. Well. He had learned to make do with what was available.

Cengh found two vacant spots on a long wooden bench along one of the tables, and gestured for Conan to sit. The Cimmerian did. He had to lean his sword against the table, for he had no scabbard. His sharp eyes had also taken note that he was the only armed man in the room. At least, the only one who had his weapon visible. He recalled Cengh's curved knife, and wondered what other loose robes might conceal.

Conan's thoughts were interrupted by a server, who sat an earthen jug down on the table, with two brass cups.

Cengh poured the wine, and offered a full cup to Conan. The Cimmerian lifted the cold brass to his lips and tilted it back. The cold wine flowed.

"This is good," Conan said. In fact, it was the best wine he had ever tasted.

Cengh smiled and refilled the empty cup. "We manage a passable vintage now and then."

A second server arrived, bearing a steaming platter. This was placed in front of Conan, who looked at it with interest. There were several small fish on the plate, and the aroma rising from them was pleasing.

Cengh produced his knife, and used it to split one of the fish along its length, revealing a long row of bones. He pried up one end of the row and peeled the entire strip away, discarding it on the empty end of the platter. "This is the best way," Cengh said. "The fish are local, caught in the mountain streams, and it is best to remove the bones, lest they stick in your throat."

Conan nodded. He had the trick. He picked up one of the fish, split the hot flesh with his fingers, and dug the thin central spine and attached bones out with one horny thumb. Then he popped most of one half of the fish into his mouth.

"This, too, is good," he managed between bites. And again, it was more than passable. The flavor was excellent, the consistency enough to provide resistance to chewing. He began to see how the priests might survive without meat. This was hardly the roots and berries he had feared.

Conan and Cengh fell to the business of eating. The platters kept coming, and after a dozen of the fish, Conan's hunger was assuaged. There was sufficient wine to mitigate his thirst, as well. Civilization did have its contents, he had to admit.

Skeer sat several tables over in the vast dining hall, near where one of the torches cast bright, flickering light upon the diners. He ate methodically, for nourishment rather than pleasure. Food was nothing, drink brought him no joy. No, Skeer's real passion came from two things: women, and the smoke of the hemp-weed. Neither of those was available in the Temple That Will Not Fall. Either of his desires was a delight; both together were as much as Skeer could wish to enjoy.

Occasionally, Skeer would cast a glance at the messenger priest and his barbarian companion. The latter ate with little regard for delicacy, and Skeer would have held him in total contempt, save for the air of alertness about him. Barbarians paid more attention to their surroundings than did civilized men, and the spy would not relish having to follow that muscular giant. Those cold blue eyes were too sharp; even Skeer's quick glances triggered some kind of atavistic response in the man. The barbarian was aware of being watched, of that the spy was certain.

Skeer went back to his meal. The barbar was of no consequence. At this point, neither was the messenger priest. What Neg the Malefic's agent needed to know he knew; it was only a matter of a few days until he could finish his mission here. When he was done, Neg's gratitude would enable Skeer to buy all the women and hemp he wished. Certainly something to look forward to, he thought.

Conan awoke with the coming of dawn. The quarters Cengh had provided were hardly luxurious; still, the room was clean, the straw mattress firm and free of vermin, and the blankets warm. A look through the small window showed that many of the priests were already about on the narrow streets, ahead of the cock's crow.

The Cimmerian youth stretched and moved to the dining hall. There seemed to be no exchange of coin for goods and services here, and Conan wondered at how well the communal living seemed to work.

The tables were laid with cheeses, boiled chicken eggs, and various fruits, along with loaves of hard black bread. Conan helped himself, washing down his meal with draughts of the priests' excellent wine. He felt much refreshed, and ready to continue his journey to Zamora.

Cengh met Conan at the exit of the dining hall. The priest carried a leather scabbard. "Ah, you are up. Have you dined?"

"Only just finished."

"Good. I thought this might make carrying your sword somewhat easier." He offered the sheath to Conan.

The brawny Cimmerian took the scabbard and examined it. It was of some rough, knobby leather, triple-stitched, with thick welting where sharp edges would touch the insides. Conan inserted the blade of his sword slowly to the guard, then jerked the weapon free. The leather hissed at the iron, but did not impede its release. A well-made sheath, and he said as much to Cengh. After a moment, a second comment arose in Conan's mind.

"If you do not kill animals, how came you by the leather for this?"

Cengh smiled, and nodded. "Why, you yourself provided it."

Conan looked at the sheath. The leather did look familiar. After a moment, he had it. "The stith."

"Indeed."

"But it was killed only two days past."

"It has been retrieved and utilized. We do not kill if we can help it, but neither do we waste anything."

"How came the leather to be tanned so quickly?"

"We have a . . . special process."

Magic was what Conan heard in the priest's undertone. He did not press the question further. Instead, he said, "I consider that we are quits on any debts, Cengh."

The priest said, "I consider my life worth more than I have given, but I accept your judgment, Conan of Cimmeria."

"I shall be on my way, then."

"Perhaps you would like to see our weapon training before you depart?"

Conan considered this. Zamora would surely wait another day or two; besides, he had a young man's curiosity and Cengh's skill with his stick had been impressive. "Aye, I would like that."

"Come, then."

Conan resheathed the sword and followed Cengh.

The man was old, his hair and beard like snow, yet he stood tall and straight within his gray robes, facing a man at least forty winters his junior. Both men held short wooden canes in two-handed grips, and each stood with his weapon tip pointing at the other's throat. The younger man was stripped to a loincloth, and his frame was well covered with muscle.

The younger man shifted his stance in quick dancing steps, this way and that, moving to within an armspan of the older man, then backward, bouncing on his feet lightly.

Conan had once seen one of the serpent-killing rodents brought to Cimmeria from far Vendhya. The owner had placed the ratlike creature in a pit with one of the hooded serpents whose bite brought quick death. This young man danced around the older man as the rodent had danced around the snake. In the end, for all its deadliness, the snake had been killed itself.

The older man shifted only enough to keep his attention focused on the younger, his movements deliberate but economical.

If asked, Conan would have wagered on the younger man to win the match. He was faster, undoubtedly stronger, and more aggressive. From the way he moved, he was no stranger to this kind of training fight. He had the edge, for the old man had demonstrated none of these qualities—

The younger man attacked. He leaped forward, raised his cane overhead, and snapped it down sharply, as if to split the older man's white forelock and the head beneath it. It was a fast strike, but hard, and had it landed, it would have knocked the old man senseless, or worse.

The old man shifted his body a hair to his left, moving slowly, it seemed to Conan, and whipped his own cane up and down in a shallow curve.

The young man's stroke missed cleanly.

The old man's cut took the other on the side, smacking loudly into a rib. The white-haired man danced a short step farther away and turned, his cane again raised to the other's throat. The young man recovered and turned to face his opponent.

After a moment, the two men relaxed, and smiled at each other.

Ho, Conan thought, sometimes the slow serpent kills the quick rat! He realized he had just learned something important. That the old man had not obviously shown his skill sooner did not mean he was without any. Impressive.

"Come and meet Oblate Kensash," Cengh said.

The old man was showing his opponent the manner of his strike, when Conan and Cengh approached.

"This is the man I spoke of," Cengh said.

"Ah," Kensash said, "the outland swordfighter. Cengh has spoken highly of your skill."

"And I have just seen yours," Conan replied.

Kensash shrugged. "Malo is my best student. Malo, this is Conan, of whom you have heard."

Malo, Conan could see, was unimpressed with whatever stories he had been told. He smirked at Conan, looking pointedly at his long black hair and darkly tanned skin. He said, "You seem fairly strong, outlander. Perhaps you would engage in a match with me?"

"I do not know the rules of your game."

"Game?" Malo bristled. "Men have died playing this *game*! No rules, save to win!"

Conan looked at Kensash. The old man wore a sad smile. "Sometimes Malo is impetuous. You are a guest, and not a student. You need not fight."

Conan grinned. "Let Malo teach me this stick game."

Kensash tendered his cane to Conan, who weighed it in his hands, swung it a few times to get the feel, and nodded at Malo. "When you are ready."

Malo grinned wolfishly and danced back two steps, to bring his cane into guard position.

Conan stood relaxed, his own weapon hanging loosely in one hand by his side.

Malo seemed impatient. "Raise your weapon! Protect yourself!"

"No need," Conan said.

That enraged Malo. He leaped at Conan and swung his cane at the Cimmerian's head. Conan stepped in toward his attacker and caught the moving stick with his left hand. The look of puzzlement on Malo's face changed to shock as Conan brought his stick first against Malo's side and then against his head. Malo dropped, stunned.

Kensash laughed, and Conan's own smile was unforced.

Malo managed to reach his feet. "You cheated! If I had been using a real sword, you would have lost your hand grabbing it!"

Conan said, "Had you been using a real sword, I would

not have been so foolish as to clutch at it. You were using only a stick.''

"But it is supposed to represent a real blade!"

"Then consider that my bare hand represented an armored gauntlet."

Malo's rage would have continued, but Kensash waved him to silence. "Would you care for a match with an old man, Conan?" he asked softly.

"Aye."

The brawny Cimmerian faced the old master. For several moments neither man moved. Then Conan shifted his stance slightly to the left.

Kensash adjusted his own feet a hair, no more.

Conan moved a shade to his right.

Kensash duplicated the motion.

After a series of such moves and countermoves, Conan knew that no matter what he did to prepare for an attack, the old man would be ready for him. To hit at this opponent was to invite instant retaliation. The Cimmerian way was to attack, and Crom take the consequences, but Conan knew that such an attack on this particular enemy would result in mutual slaying, did they both wield real swords. He was brave, but he was not insensitive to his instincts. Skill could balance bravery, were it enough, and Kensash was the most skillful swordsman Conan had ever faced.

The young Cimmerian lowered his cane and nodded at the old master.

Kensash returned Conan's nod. "You are wise beyond your years, Conan of Cimmeria. Should you elect to stay, I would be honored to teach you my small learnings."

"Nay, Oblate, not small. But my path lies elsewhere."

As Conan and Cengh left the training yard, the Cimmerian could feel the gaze of the frustrated Malo burning into his spine.

*   *   *

Tuanne walked, her feet shod in new boots, her body covered with new breeches and tunic, under a warm cloak of soft fur. The man who had provided these things had considered himself fortunate in the exchange. He had desired her, had met her terms, and made payment before he had ever touched her. The grave-chill of her flesh had turned his thoughts from lust to fear. He was, Tuanne knew, glad to be rid of her. So now the beautiful zombie walked the southern fork of the High Brythunian Road, traveling east toward her goal.

There was no way to know how far she must journey, nor how long it would take. She had no need of food, nor of rest, and she would continue as long as it took.

She had nothing if not time.

Four

In the bowels of Neg the Malefic's temple was a room unlike any of those surrounding it. This chamber held within its polished white marble walls a spire of pure quartz crystal, half the height of a man and as thick as a man's thigh. The top of the crystal had been sheared flat, and a hollow scooped from the transparent mineral, a space no larger than a child's fist. Nothing else occupied the dustless white floor, save the spire. On the gleaming walls were set carven crystal sconces, each bearing several special, slender tapers that burned smokelessly, casting smooth yellow light to every corner. The room was the antithesis of the remainder of the temple; it was clean and light and pure. Each hour, five of the Men With No Eyes came and wiped each surface carefully, to maintain that purity.

Neg strode into the chamber and observed the crystal spire. The room existed as a focus for the talisman he sought; when he had the Source of Light, it would rest in the spire of crystal. Once properly utilized, the immense powers held in the fetish would flow, and Neg would receive them. It was a secret he had stumbled upon during his questionings of the restored dead.

Neg smiled at the thought. Yes. He ranked among the highest in his control of necromantic energies, but there were limits. Once bathed in the energies of the Source of Light, he would be paramount in that rank. Strange, that such dark energies could come from something that seemed so opposite. But it was not his philosophy to ponder the "why" of such a thing, only the "how." It was enough that light and dark could be mixed to produce the results he sought. Power. Ultimate control of the dead. With a wave of his newly augmented hand, Neg would be able to raise a legion of dead to command; a second wave would put them back into eternal slumber just as easily. In battle his troops would be invincible; more, each living soldier who fell would become his thrall instantly. How unnerving that would be, to suddenly see one's battle companion rise from death to become an enemy!

It would be only a matter of a short time. Soon, Skeer would fetch that which he had been sent to collect. Soon, he would travel back to the temple of the Men With No Eyes and present the prize to his master. And soon, Neg the Malefic would become Neg the Omnipotent.

Abruptly, Neg spun, his robes flaring out, and stalked from the shining chamber. As he walked the darker hall, he saw the Men With No Eyes come to maintain the polish of the waiting chamber. Good. Good . . .

Conan made ready to depart from the Temple That Will Not Fall. He was much refreshed, and somewhat better supplied than he had been before meeting Cengh. Along with the new sheath for his blade, he now bore a pack filled with smoked fish and dried leathery strips of fruit, enough for several days sustenance. He had watched the old swordmaster practice for a time, and had learned from his observations. It was tempting to stay and enjoy this easy life, but his urge to travel would not be denied. Shadizar called.

The Cimmerian had taken his leave of Cengh and begun wending his way through the narrow streets of the temple city, when he nearly stumbled upon something that made him pause.

Crouched behind a crate of refuse was a priest. The hiding figure appeared to be watching a second priest who looked travel-worn and dusty as he made his way along one of the minor thoroughfares. More interesting to Conan was the fact that the crouching priest clutched a short dagger in one slim hand, ready to strike. Ho, an assassination?

The knife-wielding figure suddenly spun and spied Conan watching him. The Cimmerian caught a glimpse of the face under the cowl. It looked familiar, that face, young and almost girlish—

The priest sprang for Conan, knife lifted as if to stab.

There was no time to pull his sword. Conan shifted to his left, a quick, sliding step, and swung his knotted fist overhead. The hard edge of his compacted palm smacked into the attacker's wrist, knocking the knife free of its owner's grasp. The priest cursed in a high voice and tried to dart away. Conan lunged and caught a handful of robe. He jerked hard, and the priest lost his footing and tumbled to the ground, sprawling onto his back. Before he could move, Conan dropped to his knees astride the fallen priest, pinning his arms. The Cimmerian pushed the cowl away.

And beheld the face of a woman.

Her hair was hacked off short, shorter than Conan's

own, but her face was not merely that of a girlish male. He
knew a woman when he saw one. But to be certain, he slid
one hand along the fallen "priest's" chest, and discovered
the soft swelling of a female breast.

This gesture did not please the woman. She renewed her
efforts to escape, and cursed Conan through gritted teeth.

"Ignorant savage beast! Mitra take your manhood!"

Conan grinned. A spirited woman, to curse a man who
held her so. Aloud, he said, "Who are you? Why did you
try to stab me?"

"Dog, son of a dog, eater of offal, get off me!"

Conan nodded. He clamped one powerful hand around
the girl's wrist, arose from his knees, and regarded her.

"Release me!"

"When you answer my questions."

"I shall scream!"

"Oh? And show the good priests that a woman has
defiled their temple?"

That shut her up. She took several deep, sighing breaths,
and regarded Conan more closely. As she did, he remembered where he had seen her before. On the day he had
arrived, she had been picking over fruit on the main street.
He had thought that one of the priests looked less than
mannish.

Apparently, she decided that screaming was not in her
best interests.

"Well?"

"That priest has something that belongs to me," she
said. "I sought to recover it."

"By slaying him?"

"No. I would have used the dagger to ensure the return
of my property, no more."

"Then why attack me?"

"I thought you meant to stop me."

"Not I," Conan said. "I was merely passing."

"Then release me, so that I might finish my business. This is no concern of yours."

"It became my concern when you tried to skewer me."

"Barbaric fool! I *must* get to that priest before he reaches the Highest Oblate! I am sorry I mistook your intent. Please!"

Conan considered it. He had no responsibility to the priests and it was not his business, true enough. He released his grip.

Without pausing, the young woman ran to her fallen dagger, snatched it up, and sprinted from the alley.

Conan had but a brief moment before he heard her yell. She could not have reached the priest in that time. His curiosity piqued, he strode to the mouth of the alley and cast a glance after the ersatz priest.

If seeing the girl had been interesting, what he now saw was much more so: two priests stood and wrestled in the street a hundred yards distant, one bearing a short blade that glittered in the morning's golden sunlight. A third priest lay on the dusty street, a bloody stream running from his back to stain both robe and dust crimson. And the woman ran toward the two fighting men, her own knife held ready to strike.

As Conan watched, the priest with the knife drove that weapon home into the belly of the other; the wounded man clutched at his entrails and fell, red seeping between his fingers. The assassin turned to the other fallen man and ripped the bleeding man's purse from his belt. He checked it, and seemed satisfied. He then spotted the running woman and turned to flee. In a moment, he was gone, into the maw of a nearby alley. The woman veered away from the fallen men after the assassin, but he had several seconds head start. If he knew the streets, it would be unlikely that she would catch him.

It was not his business, but Conan walked to the fallen priests, curiosity running stronger than before. As he neared the stabbed men, he recognized one of them.

The belly-stabbed man was Cengh.

Suddenly this did concern the Cimmerian. Cengh was his friend. Rage enveloped Conan in a flash.

"Cengh!"

The priest coughed. "C-C-Conan. I thought you g-gone."

"Let me see the wound."

Cengh shook his head. "You cannot help. I am mortally stabbed." Cengh coughed again, and the blood flowed stronger between his fingers.

"Who did this? Why?"

"The S-S-Source of . . . Light. He t-took it."

"Who?"

The dying priest shook his head again. "I do not know him. One of Neg's hirelings. You—you must . . . recover it, Conan. Otherwise Neg will, he will . . ." Cengh coughed again, a racking, shuddering movement that ended in blood-spitting.

"Speak, Cengh! Who is Neg? Where can I find him?"

A look of peace flowed over the man's features then, and he went slack in Conan's arms.

Conan's rage flamed higher. Dead!

The young Cimmerian stood, his fists knotted tightly into hammers, his mighty chest rising and falling with his breaths. He had known Cengh but a short time, but the man had been his friend, had fed and clothed him, had shared danger with him. Shadizar could wait. Somebody was going to pay for this.

Somebody was going to pay dearly for this.

Skeer made his way to the main gate quickly, after losing his pursuer. The appearance of the small, knife-wielding priest and the barbarian had been a surprise, but in the end, they mattered not. He had the talisman. In a few moments, he would be clear of the temple and on his way, with no more than a week or ten days journey ahead of him. Neg would be pleased, and Skeer would soon be rich.

Conan picked a spot on the trail out of sight of the main temple gate, a place narrow enough so anyone attempting to pass him could not do so without being seen. He crouched in the shelter of one of the scraggly bushes and waited.

He did not doubt that the assassin would leave the temple with his booty. If he had been quick enough, Conan thought, he might have beaten the killer to this point. If so, then the man was dead. On the other hand, if the cutthroat had gotten out ahead of him, waiting here only gave him a greater lead.

The Cimmerian decided he would wait for what he thought sufficient time, and if the false priest did not appear, then he would see if he could pick up his trail farther down the mountain. Failing in that, he would inquire after someone Cengh had called ''Neg.'' The hireling would eventually return to his master, and *both* could be recipients of Conan's ire.

The cold scratched with sharp claws at Conan through his cloak, but he ignored it. Chill winds ruffled his square-cut mane and brought moisture to his fiery blue eyes, but he paid them no worry, either.

An hour after he had begun his vigil, a solitary figure dressed in gray robes approached Conan's hiding place, coming from the city.

Conan grinned wolfishly and picked his sword up from the rock against which it leaned. He had removed it from the sheath early on, so that even the whisper of leather against iron would not betray his position when the time came. He slipped from the boulder upon which he had perched and gathered his energies to spring. A bit closer, come a bit closer. . . .

Conan leaped from concealment and brandished his broadsword, ready to behead the cowled figure. "Prepare to join your cursed gods, assassin!"

The robed figure backed away quickly and raised one hand in a gesture meant to halt Conan. "Wait!" came the voice. "You are mistaken!"

Even as he stalked forward, ready to decapitate the speaker, Conan recognized the voice. Even as she quickly pulled the cowl back to reveal her face.

The young woman from the alley.

Conan lowered the sword, disgusted. "You."

"What are you doing here?" she asked.

"Waiting for the man who assassinated my friend. Consider yourself lucky you are not him."

She had no answer for that. But after a moment, she said, "I fear you will wait forever for Skeer. I had to wait for my chance to slip from the temple—the murders have caused the city to be sealed. If he is inside, the priests will find him. If without, I fear he has already made his way past this point."

Conan fastened on the name she spoke. "Skeer, you said?"

She shook her head, as if she had just realized she had spoken too much.

Conan raised his blade again. "I will have what you know of this, woman. If it was not my business before, it is now. Speak!"

"You would not kill a woman?"

"Mayhaps not. But there are other ways to obtain information."

That threat seemed to shake her. She sighed. "Very well. I shall tell you. We are both bent on the same business, that of revenge."

Conan waited.

"I am called Elashi. I come from the desert region of Khauran; my people are nomads, and have wandered the wastes for at least a hundred generations. The one you seek is called Skeer, and he is in the service of a black necromancer."

"That would be Neg," Conan said.

"You know of him?"

"Nay, only the name."

Elashi continued her story. "My father, Lorven, was chief of our tribe. Neg had him slain. A valuable . . . object was taken. I seek to avenge my father and retrieve the stolen property."

"Have you no brothers? Vengeance is a man's job."

Her eyes flashed then, and Conan saw the anger rise to her face from deep within. "I am firstborn! My brothers tend their beasts and wives! It is the eldest who must do such duties!"

"And this 'valuable object'—would it be called the Source of Light?"

This statement shook her, literally. "How did you know that?"

"A dying man's legacy."

She waited a moment before proceeding. "Aye, it carries death with it, I think. My father found it in the ruins of an ancient city uncovered by the shifting sands. He was killed for it, and those who killed him died in turn. You saw what happened to the priest who recovered the talisman after that."

"The object is cursed?"

She sighed again. "Perhaps. It is filled with power. Some arcane magic sleeps within, according to the shaman of our tribe. He could not divine its function."

Conan felt uneasy about this revelation. Magic was better left alone, in his experience. Those who dabbled in witchery often became ensnared by it in ways they had not foreseen.

"Why have you not gone directly to this Neg?" Conan asked. " 'Twould seem simpler."

"Nay. He commands power. One cannot just approach him directly. I thought to take that which he seeks and use it to gain admittance. He would see Black-Souled Set Himself to obtain the Source of Light. Once within his guard, I will kill him."

Conan thought about that. A complicated plan, too indirect for his tastes, but it might work.

"What now? You have lost your chance."

Her face hardened. "I know Skeer's visage, and to where he travels. I shall catch up with him."

The young Cimmerian regarded the woman. She was somewhat older than he, perhaps by three or four winters, and her face was attractive enough. He had reason to know she was very womanly under her priestly robes. And yet, despite her sex, she was a woman of deadly resolve. He had never met such a one before, and it attracted him. He was a loner, but he saw the common goals.

He said, "I have no use for your talisman, but I would see this Skeer and his master cross into the Gray Lands. Perhaps we can travel together."

She regarded him for a moment. "Aye, perhaps. If our common goal is all you desire."

Conan was quick to take her meaning. In truth, the thought of bedding her had crossed his mind; but, if she was uninterested, he had no problem with that. He did not force himself on women—there had never been need of that.

"Aye. Then let us depart and locate our quarry. He gains even as we speak."

The Cimmerian and the woman of the desert turned and started down the mountain.

Five

The High Brythunian Road was, in the best of seasons, a desolate place. Even when the sun warmed the lower lands to the heat of a man's blood, cold shrouded the mountain passes with permanent blankets of snow. Narrow paths were kept clear in the summer by the tramp of travelers' boots and mounts, but winter saw thickening of the white overlay to depths thrice the height of a tall man. In the fields far below, the crops were ripening toward the harvest moon. Winter had yet to blow his icy breath along the High Road, but his younger sister, Autumna, had sent warning chills of her own. Her winds carried cold, but no snow, at least.

It was along this windswept path that Tuanne trudged. She had long ago ceased worrying about the cold. It was a constant, no less than night and day, and she bore it stoically.

Ahead, according to directions she had received, lay a small village. This nameless place squatted at a juncture that virtually ensured that travelers from either direction would stop for rest or refreshment. She felt very strongly that the thing she sought approached the village from the opposite direction; the emanations of magic energy touched her with feathery fingers. If she could reach the village before the bearer of the magical device, she could set a snare for Neg's agent. Care would have to be taken; while she was impervious to death in the ordinary sense, the magic she sought to use to bring release for others might release her too soon if wielded improperly. That must not happen. She must collect the talisman, and she must return to free her zombie kin.

From ahead there came the sudden cough of a mountain cat. The sound caused her to break stride for a moment. She was not armed, at least not with weaponry that animals would respect. She knew fear, then. To be eaten by a beast—would that affect zombie charms against true death? Would she still be somehow alive in the belly of a great cat? She shuddered at the thought.

The cat slunk from behind an outcropping of cold, gray granite, belly low to the ground, its tail twitching.

Tuanne stopped and stood very still, watching the animal. She could not outrun it, there was no point in trying. If it came for her, there was little she could do.

The wind blew from behind her, toward the lion.

The cat stopped its stalk all of a moment, and Tuanne saw it wrinkle its nostrils as it caught her scent. It roared at her then, and she jumped. But the sound was not one of intention to attack; no, rather, it sounded a note of something she could not quite identify: frustration, perhaps. Or maybe it was . . . fear. For the great cat, easily twice her size, began to back away, watching her warily. When it had moved nearly to the granite outcrop, it turned and leaped, vanishing in a heartbeat.

So, she thought. Even a beast recognizes the stench of

unnaturalness and refuses to feed upon it. Her curse was, she supposed, a blessing in this case. But it brought her little joy. To be such that a hungry predator would flee was not a thing in which one would rejoice.

Sighing, Tuanne started walking along the trail once more. Night stole upon her quietly, but she only slowed to be certain of her tread. Darkness held few dangers for a zombie. Fewer now, it seemed, than before . . .

Skeer was cold and tired and more than a little hungry. He had left the monastery in a great hurry, and the horse he had cleverly hobbled for his escape had somehow managed to slip its bonds before he reached it. The missing horse carried his food and blankets as well, and there was nothing for it but to move as quickly as he could on foot. A return to the monastery for a mount and supplies would be the epitome of idiocy as well as quick suicide.

Ah, well. The village lay just ahead another hour or so. He had money, he could feast, rest indoors, and mayhaps even purchase feminine company to warm his bed. True, he would have to depart with the rising sun, upon a mount, he hoped. The priests were apt to be more than a little irate at the killings and theft, and pursuit would surely follow. Fortunately, more than one path led away from the monastery, once the major trail juncture was attained, and he hoped the false signs he had left indicating his flight elsewhere would be taken as valid. Such a fortunate happening would buy sufficient time that his pursuers would never catch him. He could afford the stop, certainly. They could not track him at night, certainly.

Darkness laid its ebon shroud upon the cliffs, but he was nearly there. He would be at the village soon, and the lights of the place shined ahead of him, beckoning.

*   *   *

"Surely he went this way," Elashi said. She gestured at the left-hand path that wound toward the south.

"I think not," Conan said.

"I am a woman of the desert," she said, "and not some simpering tavern slut with slack wits! I can read trail signs as well as any man in my tribe, and here they are so obvious a one-eyed *goat* could see them. That broken branch, used to slow the slide—see the way the dirt has been disturbed?—and the rocks kicked loose from their beds, there and there"—she pointed at the gravel as she spoke—"these things tell the tale. He passed this way, slipped upon the damp earth, and may as well have left us a message telling us to follow him!"

"Perhaps he did," Conan said. He pointed to the right-hand path. "I shall go this way." He started along the trail. He did not look back. After a moment he heard Elashi's footsteps padding up behind him.

Her voice, when she spoke, was angry.

"Barbarian, have you no sense? I have explained the signs to you! And yet you ignore them! Why do you behave this way?

Conan kept walking, but he spared her a glance. "This one you call Skeer is not a careless man," he finally said. "Many places along the upper trail were more treacherous, and yet he left no sign in half a dozen places where you lost your balance and slid and I nearly did so. For him to slip here, at such a simple and crucial turning, would seem unlikely."

"What are you saying?"

"That perhaps he did leave the signs, but deliberately."

She thought about that for a moment in silence. Then, "But what if you are wrong?"

He shrugged. "I have been wrong before. It will not kill me in this instance."

She did not speak to this, but continued to walk alongside him.

Tuanne attained the village and found what proved to be the single inn. The portly innkeep kept smiling nervously at her, as if both attracted and repelled. He answered her question through dry lips.

"Nay, mistress, none other than yourself have sought lodging this evening."

She nodded. It confirmed her sense of where the talisman was: close, but not yet here.

"I wish a room. And I will sit in the common room for a while, by the fire. Bring wine."

"Y-yes, mistress."

The man scuttled to fetch the wine as Tuanne moved to sit at a rude table set near the dwindling embers. The place was smoky and more than a little dirty, and the guttering of several fat lamps added as much to the smoke as to the light.

Several men sat drinking at the rough-cut tables: two who seemed Brythunian by dress and manner; one hawk-faced and dusky-skinned man who might be of the Stygian mid-class; a fourth who wore dark furs over darker skin, and might be Kushian or perhaps a Keshanite. A skinny woman with dirty-blond hair stood near the first pair and laughed too loudly at their jokes; likely she was the village trull, to judge from her clothing. She wore a simple thin shift and obviously nothing beneath it.

The men cast hungry glances at Tuanne as she seated herself. Some smiled and tried to lock glances with her, but she ignored them. The dark man made a sign against

evil, and looked quickly away. Perceptive, that one. The
trull seemed merely to resent the competition.

The innkeep arrived with the wine. Tuanne made no offer
to pay, and he hesitated only a moment before scurrying
away. She touched the earthen cup, twirling it upon the
table, but did not drink. Mortal food and drink held nothing for her, neither taste nor sustenance. The wine served
merely as an excuse, for appearance only. She would sit
here and await Neg's lackey.

Her plan was simple enough: she would attempt to lure
the man to her room. Failing that, she would follow him to
his room, or elsewhere, and using the stone she bore
within her belt pouch, she would bludgeon the man into
insensibility and capture the talisman.

He was coming. She could feel it.

She toyed with the wine cup, and waited.

Skeer entered the inn and, within a moment, spied the
pale and beautiful woman sitting alone by the dying fire.
How could such a one as that be alone? Were the men
seated in the room all lacking in essential maleness? At
the sight of the woman, Skeer immediately felt his own
manhood stir. Food could be ordered, and would be, and
drink to chase the chill from his bones, but he must speak
to the woman as soon as possible; else she might disappear—
surely she was some mystical creature from a delightful
dream?

He said as much to her as he sat in the chair across the
table from her. Her smile told him his attentions were not
unwelcome. It was going to be a much better night than he
had dared hope for; this was a woman to remember!

He spoke of himself as he ate the half-raw pork and
stale bread the innkeep sat before him. Most of his speech

consisted of lies, including the name he gave, his place of birth, and his occupation. He knew how to present himself in the best light to a skeptical woman; he had practiced it many times. It hardly seemed necessary with this gorgeous creature. Aside from what seemed a certain . . . coolness, she smiled at all his crude jokes, and seemed to hang upon every falsehood he devised. He washed both bread and lies down with draughts from the bottle of wine, and soon felt both warmer and more amorous. This woman drank little, but it hardly seemed to matter—she seemed perfectly willing to follow his lead without the assistance of the grape.

"I was thinking," he said, "that perhaps you might accompany me while I engage a room for the night."

Again, that cool and stimulating smile from her. "I have already taken a room," she said. "Perhaps you would care to . . . share it with me?"

"By Mitra, I would like nothing better! Come, let us go there."

"Wouldn't you like to finish your wine first?"

"We shall take the bottle with us. And another, for good measure." He could hardly believe his fortune. He would not even have to pay for the room.

He stood, wobbled but a little, and extended a hand to assist her—what was her name again?—ah, well, no matter—to her feet.

"Your hand is like ice," he said, when he felt her touch.

"Surely a man such as yourself can bring warmth to it?"

He grinned. "Aye. I can warm all manner of things, my lady."

Tuanne followed Neg's minion down the narrow hallway toward the room indicated by the leering innkeeper. A stub of a taper provided flickering shadows and only a feeble glow against the darkness. They entered the unlit room, and she smiled in the gloom. It would be easier in the darkness. She reached into her purse and touched the smooth stone nestled there.

Sparks danced just ahead of her, accompanied by the *chink!* of flint on steel.

"What are you doing?" she asked.

"Lighting a taper, lady."

"Why? You have no need of eyes for this particular engagement."

The sparks danced upon the wick of the candle he held, and a small flame glowed into life. "Ah, my lady, such beauty as yours must be seen as well as touched. Here we are. Come, remove those concealing garments and allow me to feast my eyes."

Tuanne hesitated only a moment. He seemed more alert than he had in the common room, and he could see her too easily. Better not to chance an attack now—he had the talisman upon his person, and she was uncertain as to what might happen if she were exposed to it incorrectly. In a few moments, when he was either occupied or sated, the timing would be better. It did not matter if she did that which he wished. She began to disrobe, removing her boots and breeches, then her vest and shirt. In a minute, she stood naked before him, the candlelight glimmering over her form. Her skin made the palest ivory seem dark, even in the dim light, and her body was as lush and rich as any living woman's.

The man sucked in a startled breath. "You are more beautiful than I imagined," he said, his voice hoarse. Quickly, he began to remove his own clothing. He took special care with his purse, and Tuanne knew this was where he had hidden that which she sought. Once it was safely out of his grasp, she could proceed.

"Come here," he ordered. He lay back on the pallet and extended his arms to her.

Tuanne smiled and moved toward him. Unseen, her foot nudged her own purse toward the edge of the pallet, so that the stone within would only be a short reach away.

At the base of the rickety stairs leading to the inn's sleeping quarters, Conan and Elashi stood, talking in low whispers to the innkeeper.

"My patrons deserve their privacy," the portly man said. But he rubbed his thumb across the fingertips of his left hand several times, as though feeling an imaginary coin.

In answer, Conan dropped his own hand to touch the hilt of his sword. There was no need for speech, for the innlord took that meaning quickly enough. "Ah, the third room from the end. He—he is with a woman."

"Return to your business," Conan ordered.

As the innkeep shuffled quickly away, Conan started up the stairs. Elashi started to follow, but he held out his hand. "No. I shall deal with the killer of my friend."

"But the Source of Light—"

"I have no need of magical devices. I shall bring it to you when I am done."

"How can I trust you?"

Conan's blue eyes smoldered in the faint light. "You have my word."

They stood silently for a moment, and when he turned to ascend the stairs, she stood her own ground.

Before he reached the hallway at the stairtop, he drew

his blade. Three doors down, was it? He trod carefully, settling his not-inconsiderable weight onto each footstep as though walking upon fragile ice he wished to avoid breaking.

"By Bel, you are as cold as the pit of winter!"

Tuanne pressed herself against the man, and said, "I have been standing bare in this chilly room. A draught of wine will warm me. I'll get it."

"Hurry."

But what her hand found when it left their bed was not wine in an earthen bottle, but a stone that fit comfortably within her grip.

"What are you doing? What is that?"

He was alarmed; something in her motion must have given her away. She twisted away from him and raised the stone.

There existed a number of things he could have done, several of which would have produced results in his favor. He could have leaped from the bed and fled; he could have caught Tuanne's wrists and struggled, for her strength was no more than that of a mortal woman; he could have ducked the striking hand. What he did instead, however, was to snatch at his clothing for the knife he carried. In a smooth and practiced motion, he thrust the short blade up at the woman, sinking it to the hilt in her stomach, then jerking it free so that her blood might flow fast and freely.

Tuanne smiled as she saw the satisfaction on his face turn to horror. There was no blood, and had he managed to stay conscious for another moment, he would have seen the edges of the wound seal and vanish back into perfect whiteness. But she continued her own motion, and the stone met flesh and bone just over his ear, and his senses were clouted from him. He went limp without a sound.

Tuanne dropped the stone and arose. She spared the unconscious man a single glance, then turned toward his clothing—

Conan kicked the door so hard it flew from its hinges. He leaped into the room. Light from a single candle shined within, to reveal—

By Crom! What a woman this was!

Gloriously nude, she spun to face him.

Before she could speak, he said, "Fear not, lady. My business is with your friend there." Conan pointed with his sword. "He sleeps soundly for all this noise."

"He is not asleep, big man. He is unconscious. He sought to—to . . . take advantage of me. I managed to hit him on the head. He is a villain most foul."

"Aye, that he is, lady." He continued to stare at the woman. He had seen his share of women undraped, but none so lovely as this one. And he was young enough so that the fires ran very hot in his blood at a sight such as this.

"You have rescued me, and I am most grateful," she said. She smiled at Conan, then seemed to notice for the first time that she was naked. "Oh."

Conan did not feel as though he had done much in the way of rescue, but certainly he had no intention of arguing with this woman. She could be as grateful as she wished. He lowered the point of his sword. She moved closer. "I am called Tuanne," she said. "And what is your name, my bravo?"

"Conan. Of Cimmeria."

"Ah. One of the strong northern men."

While his attention was focused upon her, Conan's vigilance suffered. The room bore a window, covered with a thin layer of cloth. It was through this aperture that the supposedly unconscious Skeer suddenly took leave. The man leaped to his feet sans covering, and dove through the portal.

Conan leaped past the woman, uttering a curse, and would have followed, but a voice from behind stopped him.

"Hold!"

Conan spun, his sword raised.

Elashi stood in the doorway, brandishing a sword of her own. Where had she come by that? Conan wondered.

"Skeer escapes," he said, gesturing at the window.

"I will have the talisman," she said. "Give it to me."

"I do not have it," the Cimmerian began.

"Now, or I will skewer you like a pig!" She advanced, her sword leading.

Woman or not, Conan was not a man to take such a threat lightly. He moved to meet her attack. Peripherally, he noticed the woman called Tuanne scrambling to gather her clothing. He turned his attention away from her; she was no threat, but this mad desert woman might well be.

"For my father!" Elashi yelled, and lunged at Conan.

He parried her thrust with his blade, but held his own return cut. Whatever else she was, she was no swordfighter. Her balance was wrong, her strike awkward, and her footwork almost comical.

He allowed her to strike at him twice more before he slammed his own weapon into her sword, hard. The shock of it tore her grip loose, and the blade fell upon the floor with a clatter. She made as if to attack him bare-handed, and he had to move his sword quickly to avoid accidentally injuring her. She was foolish, but certainly brave.

"Stop," he said. "I yield."

"Do not make sport of me, barbarian!"

"Nay, Elashi. I am not your enemy, though you refuse to see it. Skeer left without a stitch to cover him. If he has your talisman, it still lies here."

She drew herself up. "Very well. Where?"

"Perhaps Tuanne saw it—" The brawny Cimmerian stopped speaking. Where was the beautiful woman?

"If you are looking for the harlot, she left."

Conan moved to the pile of clothes Skeer had left. He had seen, briefly, a pouch lying among them when he'd entered the room. The pouch no longer lay there.

"Well? Where is it?"

Conan said, "It seems that Tuanne has taken it."

"And *you* just let her do it."

"It was you who created the diversion," he said. "Had you not come in with your swordplay, we would have Skeer and the talisman. Now we have neither."

"Your talent for stating the obvious is wonderful, Conan. Now we have to find them both."

She turned and stalked from the room, and Conan could only shake his head. Women. What man could understand them?

Six

Whatever vestige of wine remaining within Skeer had lost its ability to fog his mind. No, the chill of the evening upon his bare skin alone would have remedied that even if he had not bounced from a low rooftop onto the hard ground outside the inn while making good his escape. His head hurt where the woman—the *zombie* woman, he corrected his thought—had clouted him with something; but far worse, he had lost the Source of Light; in the end, that would be fatal.

There was much confusion within Skeer. The woman was a zombie, certainly. He had seen enough of the creatures at Neg's beck, and he felt a fool for not recognizing her sooner. As to the massive barbarian, he recognized him from the temple. A hound sent by the priests, no doubt, and one able to recognize the false trail, as well. Not good.

Well. The hound was one thing, the zombie another. One of them had the talisman now, and he would have to determine which, and then retrieve it. He had no desire to become one of Neg's undead himself, and his failure would lead to that, not to mention a most horrible passage before reaching that loathsome state. Neg had never been accused of being merciful.

He had clothing, of a sort. A drying line yielded a coarse shirt and breeches, and a cobbler's shop with a poor lock had given him a pair of new boots that almost fit. A further foray into a merchant's shop had provided a short sword and a supply of salt.

This latter substance held no enchantment, and thus its effectiveness was sorely limited; still, it was the best he could do under the circumstance. Mixed with water and held now in a stoppered jar, the solution offered a temporary stay to the zombie, should he encounter her first. A sufficiently saline solution would paralyze one of the undead for a short time. Long enough to recover the talisman and be several hours distant before she could recover.

If she had the magical object.

It might be that the barbarian swordsman had it, which produced a different set of problems. But he had to sleep sometimes, and Skeer could forgo that pleasure to save his hide.

So, the first problem lay in figuring out which way whoever had the Source of Light would travel. The barbarian would no doubt be returning it to the Suddah Oblates for some reward, and therefore retracing the path Skeer had taken to arrive at the village. An unpleasant thought, that, to contemplate meeting with those worthies.

As for the zombie, well—who could tell what a dead woman might think? If she were one of Neg's, then she would have come from the east, opposite his own trek from the west. But why had she come at all? Had Neg sent her, not trusting Skeer's abilities? While he would not put it past the necromancer, that made little sense. But if she wanted the talisman, then she would probably wish to avoid the priests, did she know they, too, wished to possess it. So she would go the opposite way.

So, the zombie or the barbarian?

In truth, neither choice appealed greatly to Skeer. But the third choice, of eventually having to face Neg's wrath, appealed even less. And deciding wrongly of the first two would ultimately bring upon him the third.

Well. Since both the zombie and the barbarian wanted the talisman, and both had been there with it, he had to think upon which would likely prevail. As clever as he himself was, *he* had been duped by the woman. What chance would a mere barbarian lout have against the wiles of such a beauty? Little or none, Skeer figured. So, east it was.

On his way from the village, he stole a horse. Were she on foot, he would catch her before daybreak.

Tuanne kept the Source of Light encased within the thick leather of the purse so that it could not come into contact with her flesh. She felt the pull of it, a mystic call that whispered for her to touch it and be free, but her resolution remained firm. No, when she could release the others from their bondage, then she would know that freedom herself. Until then, she would ignore the siren call from the magical key.

The arrival of Conan and the woman who obviously knew him had been a near disaster. She had been lucky to escape. The Source of Light was sought by more than just herself, and she would have to be vigilant until her need for it passed. After that, she did not care who had it—as long as it was not Neg. To be called from the Gray Lands a second time would be more than she could bear.

The night and its cold enveloped her as she walked along the road, retracing her earlier path. She was tired, in a way that the living could not be tired, but she did not need sleep or food as they did. A mortal pursuer would have to rest and sup, and each moment thus wasted would advance her lead.

In the dark, Tuanne walked, feeling, for the first time in a hundred years, hope for her own future.

"We must go east," Conan said.

"I understand," Elashi said.

The big Cimmerian looked at her. Thus far, she had questioned virtually all his decisions. He did not ask, but she told him anyway.

She said, "Anyone going west will run into the priests, and thus will be taken captive. We can always check that. Anyone going east will escape, unless *we* capture them."

"Mm," he said, acknowledging her logic. "At dawn."

"Yes, we might as well use the room Skeer left for us. You sleep there." She pointed at the corner and tossed him a blanket. "I shall sleep here."

Conan shrugged.

She settled upon the bed, while the young giant moved to his assigned corner. Just as he began to drift into slumber, however, she spoke.

"Did you think she was beautiful?"

Conan came back from the edge of sleep. "Who?"

"That woman. Tuanne, you called her."

"Yes."

"You thought so? With such unhealthy white skin you thought her beautiful?"

"Yes."

"Men!"

Conan awaited further dialogue, but none came. He shrugged again and sank into blissful sleep.

As the false dawn neared, Skeer beheld his quarry trudging along the trail toward him. Ah! He had risked his neck and that of his mount by leaving the trail to circle ahead. He had been fortunate; the horse still had use of all four legs and here his risk was now repaid!

He lay in wait behind a thick-boled evergreen tree, his horse tied to another such well back from the road. The zombie's walk was listless, if steady, and she seemed to take little notice of her surroundings.

Skeer unstoppered the jar of saltwater and held the container ready. Soon . . . soon . . .

She came abreast of him. He leaped out into the road and hurled the contents of the jar at her. She threw up one hand to protect herself, but the gesture did not help. As the liquid struck her, she stiffened, and fell into a supernatural swoon.

Skeer moved to the downed figure, bent, and tore his purse from her grasp. He laughed. " 'T'would pay you not to meddle in Skeer's affairs, undead bitch." He looked at her, helpless on the dusty road. She could hear him and see him, he knew, she just could not move.

He considered dallying for a few moments, to finish that which he had desired earlier at the inn. She would not object, and he had no interest in her pleasures, in any event. It would be the work of a few moments to undress her. . . .

No. He had nearly lost the Source of Light that way earlier, and in those few moments, pursuit could draw that much closer. A pity, but he valued his life much more than any woman, no matter how comely. Riches and women by

the hundreds awaited him farther along; merely quick pleasure and risk existed here.

He turned and moved toward his tethered horse.

"Farewell, undead one."

His laugh echoed in the trees.

The sun rose and beamed down upon her, but its heat
was scant, and its light showed only cloudy skies. Tuanne
had been trying to move for hours, and not even the
smallest vibrations had she managed. She gathered her
energies once again. . . .

Under the drying crust of salt, she moved her left arm.
It was only a small motion, barely a quiver, but it meant
that the effect of the saltwater had nearly worn off. Skeer
would be far away, but once she could move, she could
follow. That single goal held everything for her.

Conan spied the woman. She seemed to be sitting in the
middle of the road, odd. He drew his sword, as did
Elashi. (The blade, she finally reported, had been lifted
from the side of a drunken man in the inn's common
room. Likely he had yet to awake and miss it. A lesson in
thievery of which the Cimmerian took note. Anyone who
could allow his sword to be stolen thusly surely had little
need of it.)

Tuanne must have heard their approach, for she turned
to look at them; still, she did not rise. Perhaps she was
injured? Good for them, Conan thought, if not for her.

Conan loomed over the sitting woman. He pointed his
sword at one shapely breast. "We'll have Skeer's purse
and that which it contains," he said.

Tuanne began to cry. Her body shook with great sobs,

and lines of tears tracked her perfect skin. She cried as
does a child who has lost her mother.

Conan found himself backing a pace away and lower-
ing his weapon. "Hear, what is this?"

The woman continued to cry. She was not especially
loud, but it was obviously founded in deepest grief.

"Stop that," the young Cimmerian said, feeling awkward. "Nobody will harm you. We want only—"

"Oh, hush, fool barbarian!" Elashi said. She had already sheathed her own sword, and now she bent to put
her arms around the crying woman. Tuanne buried her
face in Elashi's breast and continued to sob quietly. Elashi
petted the dark hair and murmured softly, "There, there."
She turned and glared at Conan. "See what you have
done."

"I? I have done?"

"Yes, you and your threats."

Conan's rage rose in his breast, but he had no focus for
the anger. He wished to slay something, but—what? A
crying woman huddling against another? He turned and
stomped to the edge of the road, hoping something would
leap out and attack him. A bear, a wolf, a demon, anything. Nothing did, however, and his frustration merely
increased.

After a few moments, Elashi called to him.

"Conan. You should come and hear this."

Tuanne had stopped crying, and with Elashi's help, had
gained her feet. Conan saw that her clothing was crusted
with some whitish powder.

"I do not have the talisman you seek," she began.
"The one you call Skeer followed me and took it."

Conan ground his teeth together. Everybody wanted this
accursed device!

"I must have it," she said.

"Why?"

She turned to answer the Cimmerian's question. "I need it to help me die."

When she finished her story, Conan could think of little to say. "You are truly a zombie?"

"I died more than a hundred years past," she said. "But I have not been permitted to take my rightful place in the land of the dead. Nor have dozens of others under Neg's thrall."

"This Neg deserves killing," he said.

"If he obtains the Source of Light, he shall be able to raise legions of dead. And he will certainly use his powers to do more evil."

Conan shrugged. "It is not my business to meddle in magical affairs. I have a debt to pay to Cengh, that is all."

"We must help her," Elashi said. Her voice was firm. .

Conan said nothing, knowing she would explain. She always did.

She did not disappoint him. "We shall catch Skeer and retrieve the Source of Light. Then, we shall travel to the crypts where the other prisoners are held and use it to free them—and her. You"—she nodded at Conan—"may then slay Neg, and I shall take the talisman back to my home."

The muscular youth shook his head.

"Is there a flaw in my plan? Is it not simple?"

"It is simple enough," Conan said.

"Then what?"

He thought about that for a moment. He *did* wish to settle the score with Skeer; and, since Neg had dispatched the killer, such settlement extended to him, as well. The plan was direct—he liked that part of it—only, the idea of traveling with two women, well, that might be more complex. It was difficult enough with one.

"Well?" Elashi demanded.

"Nothing," he said. "We shall try your plan."

"I do not see how it can fail," Elashi said.

Prudently, Conan chose not to speak to that statement.

Winter, however, did choose that moment to make his presence felt. He did so in the form of a blizzard that quickly boiled over the mountaintops, battering all beneath it with sleet, hail, and, of course, snow.

Conan knew how to deal with such weather, and immediately began to build a lean-to in the woods nearby, using his sword to trim branches and vines for the structure. Within an hour, he had shelter for the three of them, a small fire going to fight the hard chill, and a nest of evergreen boughs for added warmth.

"How long must we stay here?" Elashi asked.

"Until the storm stops."

"We do not have weather like this in the desert. How long will that be?"

He shrugged. "An hour, a day, three days. Only the gods know."

"But Skeer will escape!"

Before Conan could answer, Tuanne said in a soft voice, "Not likely. If you cannot travel, neither can he."

Elashi regarded the pale woman. "Could you travel in this storm?"

"I could, but slowly. And I would be . . . colder than usual."

The woman of the desert sighed. "Well. I suppose we shall just have to wait, and hope we do not lose his trail."

"I can locate that which he carries," Tuanne said. "He can flee, but he cannot hide, not from me."

The coldness of her voice touched Conan then, with a finger more icy than the wind blowing around them. She was beautiful, of that there was no doubt, but she was also something outside his experience. She did not look dangerous, but that she was, he also had no doubt. He put more wood on the fire against the cold, but it did not drive this particular chill from him.

Skeer's fortune had shifted into the realm of the less-than-good. When the storm started, he had pushed his mount, in an attempt to outrun it for shelter. As the snow thickened, he lost the trail. His mount stumbled and threw him, fortunately without injury to himself. Unfortunately, the horse had broken his leg. Skeer realized he was going to be stranded for the duration of the storm.

Well, he thought, as he pulled his sword and advanced on the hapless animal, at least he would not be hungry. . . .

Seven

The storm beat at the Earth with icy fists for two days and nights. Came the dawn of the third day, the sun finally reclaimed the land, sending his golden light over a world enshrouded in glistening white. Just in time, too, since the last of their provisions had been consumed.

Conan had not been idle during the blizzard. He had used his dagger to carefully carve three sets of snowshoes from green saplings. The storm had not spared the road, and the attendant cold had crusted the surface, but not to a solidity that would support the weight of a man on mere boots. Too, he had attempted to forage for food; unfortunately, he had sighted no game during the wintery onslaught. It had been left to Tuanne, who herself did not eat, to locate some tough and starchy roots upon which Conan and Elashi chewed. The Cimmerian liked this fare little—he was beginning to feel like a squirrel—but he had little choice. Better rabbit food than none at all. In any event, the storm had done its mischief, and it was now possible to depart.

71

Elashi had her doubts. "We will sink to our breasts in this accursed snow and freeze!"

"Nay," Conan said. "With these"—he waved the snowshoes—"we can stay on the surface, if we move with care."

Such a thing proved to be the case. The Cimmerian youth led the way across the mounded snows; he sank, but only a little, and his steps created small shush-shush sounds in the frigid air. Conan was a large man, and if the snow would support his weight, Elashi and Tuanne had little worry of being swallowed by the white powder.

Movement was possible, but speed other than slow was not. The young Cimmerian's breath made fog in the air as he shuffled along the road, buried now beneath half a span of fresh snow. Likely Skeer would be having no easier time of it, unless he had cleared the mountain pass before the storm had begun, and Conan contented himself with that belief. Of course, the thief and slayer did not have two women along to slow his pace; still, one made do.

At the moment that the three pursuers began to follow him once again, Skeer moved not at all; rather, he sat wrapped in a blanket, huddled next to a small fire, in magical contact with Neg. He had eaten well, but his trip would be slowed for it. And his lack of a speedy return must be explained, lest Neg chastise him for it.

It had taken no small effort to capture a snow hare. He did not need the meat, but warm blood was essential for the communicatory spell. He had no desire to utilize his own crimson essence, though that was always an option.

Contact was established. The Connection forged in magical fires became as a link between Skeer and his master.

"SPEAK."

Best move directly to the heart of things, Skeer figured. "I am delayed by a winter storm, lord. My mount is no more, and it might take some time to replace it, as there are none available nearby."

"DO YOU HAVE THAT WHICH I SEEK?"

"Be assured that I do, my lord. I shall hasten to deliver as soon as possible."

"SEE THAT YOU DO. WASTE NO TIME."

"By your command, lord."

Skeer felt the contact sunder, and he shuddered at the malign power of the necromancer that still vibrated through his soul. Neg must not find him wanting, lest his ire manifest itself as Skeer had seen it happen to others. As a master, the necromancer was powerful and generous to those who served him well. To those who served him less than successfully . . . well, 'twas better not to think of them.

The thief stood, stretched his cold ligaments, and swung his arms to hasten the circulation of blood. Best to do as he had been instructed, and waste no time.

"Do you know this route?" Conan asked.

Tuanne nodded. "Yes. We currently travel toward the four mountains known as the Death Mask. Somewhere within their valley lies Opkothard, the city of mystery. It I have never seen, and even rumors speak of it in whispers."

"Is our quarry likely to go there, do you think?" Elashi asked.

Tuanne shook her head. "Unlikely. The most direct path lies ahead. There would be no reason to detour."

"Then perhaps we can catch up to him," Elashi said.

Conan did not state his doubt of this—that Skeer had a horse and they did not. Alone, at a trot, he might maintain the pace of a mount. With these two, Conan thought it unlikely they would catch their quarry.

This was only moments before they discovered Skeer's camp, however. When he saw the remains of Skeer's ill-fated horse, the big Cimmerian was glad he had not voiced his earlier worry. The left foreleg of the animal was broken, though hardly the cause of death. Though the local vermin had been at the corpse, leaving no useful meat, Conan found a vertebra that had been cleaved in twain with a sword. Skeer had killed his mount, likely due to the broken limb. And had eaten better for it, though he walked now. Fortune had smiled upon them in that respect, at least.

"Perhaps Skeer will detour to this Opkothard after all," Conan said. "Unless he wishes to travel the remaining distance on foot. We might catch him there. Or at least obtain mounts of our own."

"Have you funds for such a purchase?" Tuanne asked.

Conan smiled. "Nay. But I have come to realize that such a state is not always an impediment."

Nightfall found the trio only half the distance they would have traveled without the encumbrance of snow; still, Skeer could travel no faster, and would hardly be gaining. Conan hurried to gather small branches from a dead tree. "We must build a fire," he said.

Elashi, as she was wont to do, remarked upon this with no small amount of superiority in her voice.

"Why do you hurry, Conan? Are you so cold?"

As if in answer, a distant howl came, echoing in the dimming light. After three heartbeats, the howl was followed by a second, then a third. A moment more, and the air seemed alive with the voice of the wild creatures.

Elashi turned to Tuanne, who moved to help Conan gather wood.

"Wolves," Tuanne said simply. "Or worse."

"Worse?"

"Dire-wolves, perhaps. Or those touched with the magic of a were."

"I don't understand," Elashi said. "A where?"

"Werewolves. Men, who when the moon is right or the magic high enough, change from human into magicked creatures. They look like wolves, and act much as natural wolves, but they are intelligent, as are men, and impervious to normal weapons."

Elashi shuddered. It was no more than another heartbeat before she was next to Conan, stripping dry twigs from the tree.

Once the fire was going, Conan felt better. Natural beasts feared fire. If these things painting the night with their songs were other than natural, he would trust to his sword. Crom gave a man courage at birth, and a strong arm and sharp blade would divest a magical beast of its head, he would wager. His dealings with magic thus far in his young life had left a bad taste upon his tongue, and he wanted no part of it.

The beastly howls grew closer. Conan noted that Elashi and Tuanne both seemed more tolerant of his closeness as the sounds drew nearer. At one point, he leaned in to add fuel to the crackling fire. When he leaned back, he felt the hips of both women touch his own brawny thighs to either side. He grinned, but it was a tiny one, more to himself than visible. There were some advantages to the night noises.

The Cimmerian spread his cloak wide. "Wrap this around you," he told the women, "so that we may share our warmth.'' In truth, with the fire roaring only a span away, he was quite warm; still, both Elashi and Tuanne seemed eager to accept.

To his right, Elashi radiated much heat of her own; but to his left, Tuanne seemed as cold as might a woman carved from marble and left out in the chill of winter. Soft, her body was, but frigid.

With his belly rumbling around the roots and tubers he had eaten and the warmth of the fire and companionship of two women, Conan felt himself slip into a doze.

He awoke to Tuanne's hurried whisper.

"Conan."

The Cimmerian's blue eyes flicked open, to see a monster facing him across the dim remains of the fire.

It was some form of wolf, but half the size of a horse, and nearly as white as the snow around it. In the faint light of the fire, the thing's bared teeth gleamed like old ivory.

Conan felt Elashi stir next to him. "Prepare to stoke the fire," he whispered. "I shall see if I can frighten it away."

The dire-wolf edged a bit nearer, watching Conan intently.

Abruptly, Conan leaped to his feet and waved his sword. "Ho, wolf!" he yelled. His voice was a harsh bass that thundered in the quiet night.

The dire-wolf jumped backward twice its length, startled, but stopped there and held its ground. Without turning around, Conan said, "Tuanne, do you think this might be one of those were-creatures of which you spoke?"

"It does not have a magical air about it, no," she replied.

"Good. Build up the fire, in case it has brothers."

The white wolf growled, a deep rumble. Its lips lifted to

show the finger-long fangs, and the ruff on its shoulders rose. Stiff-legged, it took a small step toward Conan.

The man gripped his sword's handle loosely, avoiding tension that would slow him, and began to circle to his right.

The wolf turned to follow Conan's progress. The rumble increased. Conan watched as it gathered itself for a spring.

The wolf leaped, aiming for Conan's throat. Lithely, the Cimmerian youth bounded to one side, out of the creature's path. He swung the big broadsword around and over his head, as might a man splitting wood with an axe, but kept his shoulders down, as he had been taught.

The wolf's speed was deceptive. It seemed to move slower than it actually did. Conan's swing, had it connected with the beast's neck or body, would have dealt it a killing blow. As it happened, the razored edge of the sword met instead the tip of the beast's tail, and severed it neatly.

The wolf howled and spun, but its balance was altered by the missing segment of tail. When it darted in to sink its teeth into Conan's thigh, what it found instead was the Cimmerian's cloak. Growling, it tore at the material, shaking it from side to side.

Having adjusted for his earlier error, Conan's second cut was more accurate. His blade sang in the frosty air, a cold melody of iron and blood, and the edge of the sword met the gristle and bone of the dire-wolf's neck. The contest went to the man and forged metal.

The beast's head sagged, then fell away from the body, sinking into the snow with a wet thump. An instant passed before the body of the wolf realized its fate. Then, in a single, final spasm, the body sprang sightlessly, smashing into Conan, knocking him sprawling, gouting crimson over the fallen man.

Both Tuanne and Elashi leaped toward Conan, yelling his name.

The Cimmerian giant sat up and shoved the corpse of the wolf away from him, smearing yet more of the thing's gore over his hands. Steam arose from the congealing blood, to dissipate in the night's hard cold.

"It is nothing," he said, getting to his feet.

The two women stared at him. Even Tuanne, who must have seen many sights in her unnatural lifetime, seemed amazed that Conan still lived.

"Lend me your knife," Conan said to Elashi. "Perhaps the white fur of this beast might be worth something."

Silent for once, Elashi tendered her dagger.

Conan tested the edge, found it satisfactory, and set to removing the pelt of the dire-wolf. The creature would have no more use for it. He could not tan it properly, but the wolf also had brains it would no longer need, as well. Rubbed into the inner lining of the pelt, they would help preserve it until proper methods could be used.

Eight

Neg swung his hand hard, and the back of it smacked against the face in front of him with a satisfying, if not particularly effective, slap.

The recipient of the strike held his unblinking stare without apparent pain or even interest. He was one of the Men With No Eyes, and his glassy orbs swam with swirling and tiny gray clouds that gave his face the only movement visible.

"Is she the only one?" Neg demanded.

The figure nodded once, the gesture almost a bow.

"Then you shall replace her!"

At this the figure finally showed some emotion. He backed away, raising his hands.

Neg smiled. He waved, and another pair of his sightless minions flowed toward the condemned one. They grabbed him tightly, and for a moment, it seemed as if he might resist. Abruptly, the struggles stopped, as if the man—it had once *been* a man, after all—realized the uselessness of his actions.

"Take him to the vaults. Kill him."

After the three had departed, Neg moved to observe himself in a looking glass on the nearby wall of his chamber. *Where have you gotten to, Tuanne? Not within my range of command, for I cannot feel your essence, either in the land of the living or the dead. The In-Between Lands? I could not find you, be you there, but how did you manage to leave my vaults, my pretty night-child?*

Neg's image regarded him impassively, its face hiding any emotion beneath a mask of unconcern. *It bodes ill, brother,* the image seemed to say, *for one of your thrall to escape. Such a thing has never happened before. Is your power waning? Is there some preternatural force interfering with your own? Has some trickster god inserted his verge into your affairs for reasons of his own?*

Neg turned away from the glass, disturbed by the questions of his mirror image. Such things could not be answered. She was gone, whatever the reason, and that was as much as he could ascertain at the moment.

Very well. He could deal with that aspect of the affair. Aside from the fact that Tuanne was one of his favorite slaves, there existed the matter of maintaining appearances. True, he deemed it unlikely that anyone outside his castle would ever know of her escape; still, if anyone *did* learn of it, it would seem a chink in his power. Therefore, it would behoove him to locate the woman and retrieve her as soon as possible.

He clapped his hands. Almost immediately, one of the blind priests stood before him. It was as if the man had heard the sound of Neg's hands in the air before they had slapped together, so fast was the response. Possibly he had; the cult had hearing beyond that of mortal men.

''Go and find my thrall, the one your brother allowed to

escape. Take five like yourself and go now. Do not return without her.''

The Man With No Eyes bowed, and turned away, his robes flaring with the quickness of his move.

Good, Neg thought. That chore would be settled soon. The Men With No Eyes were most tenacious. He would content himself with devising an appropriate punishment for the lovely Tuanne when she was returned to him. Something subtle, but effective.

Meanwhile, he would await the delivery of the Source of Light. Should it arrive before his priests could fetch Tuanne, that would end the matter. With the talisman's power, he could find her anywhere, Between Lands or no. His reach would be boundless.

He grinned at the thought and felt quite happy. Perhaps another rat would try to scold him as he walked the dank halls of the castle. That would be nice. He would like to use his death-gaze once again. And when he exhausted the rat supply? Well, there were always the nearby villagers. . . .

Skeer's feet bore large blisters inside his ill-fitting boots as he approached the city of Opkothard. He had caught distant glimpses of it as the trail twisted through the craggy mountains, but when he rounded the final bend that allowed him a full view, he abruptly forgot the pain in his feet.

Opkothard: it was a place of much speculation by those who had never been there. He himself had managed to survive thirty-two winters without laying his gaze upon the place, and had never felt the lack. As he stared at the city wall no more than an hour's walk ahead, he wished he did not have to see it now.

The city wall was massive, the exact color of the surrounding rock, and likely built of that same gray stone. Judging size at this distance was no easy chore, but if that ant crawling along the top was a man, then the wall scaled a height of at least twelve spans. What need had they of a barrier that high? And correspondingly thick, too, he would wager.

There was only one entrance along the unbroken gray wall, that being astride the very path upon which he now trod. The gates, themselves half the height of the wall, seemed to be of some dark red material. As he drew closer, Skeer observed that this material seemed to be iron, and the red a thin layer of rust. No invading force would burn through those portal doors!

As if any invading force could even *reach* the doors. For, as he approached, the thief saw that the path narrowed for the last segment, so that nothing wider than a single dray could traverse it. To either side, a sheer drop loomed, ending in jagged rocks far below. Just before the gates, a domino bridge finished the path. With it raised, a gap wider than five armspans would open its maw to swallow any so foolish as to try and leap it.

The Opkothardians did not wish to have uninvited company, so it would seem. And any not allowed in would have a difficult time trying to force entrance. Three or four men might march abreast along the narrow path to the drawbridge, but leaping over the gap while avoiding arrows from a phalanx of bowmen on the walls certainly did not fulfill any of Skeer's ambitions. Leave that to men without enough sense to come in out of the rain.

The guard posted above the gates must have seen Skeer approaching for the better part of half an hour, and yet he seemed to take no notice until Skeer hailed him.

"Ho, the city!"

"Yes? What would ye be needin', footman?"

"Entrance would do."

"Aye, ye would think so. For what purpose?"

Skeer had not thought of having to satisfy an examination for entrance to the city; still, his wit had never been dull on such matters. As he had walked the final steps to the gate, he had spied painted upon the rock near the rusted iron a symbol, that of a fat-bodied spider. Now Skeer paid reverence to no particular gods, though he was wont to use the names of many, usually in swearing. But he had some knowledge of this particular symbol: it represented the Nameless spider-god, a patron deity of Yezud, were he not mistaken. The Nameless had never held sway over great numbers in the way that Mitra, Bel, or even Set had done; still, the Nameless had his worshipers. For his sign to be so prominently displayed upon the otherwise graffitiless wall likely meant something of import.

"Well, footman? Did the devil take your tongue?"

"There could be many reasons for my journey here, fellow man, but as it happens, I came to pay my respects to Him With No Name, whose form carries legs eight in number."

"Eh? Why didn't ye say so in the first place? Welcome, pilgrim, to Opkothard. May the Nameless look upon you with favor."

"And may He look upon you as you deserve, as well, friend," Skeer said. *And I hope he sucks your juices out through your eyes, fool.*

The right half of the massive gate swung outward enough to admit a single man, making in the short journey a screech that would have given a demon pause. Skeer congratulated himself in his quickness of thought, as he moved into the mysterious city that liked spiders.

When Conan and his two companions approached the city gate to Opkothard, the shadows stretched long, as the sun settled for his nightly rest. The Cimmerian had seen other walled cities, though none with such an imposing fence as this one.

"Ho," the watchman called down from the wall top, "state what business ye have in Opkothard." There sounded an arrogance in his voice that instantly grated on the brawny Cimmerian.

Conan was tempted to yell to the watch that such business was his own, but he held his tongue. While he could easily clamber over the wall, being a Cimmerian bred to the mountains, the two women might not fare so easily.

Before he could speak, however, Tuanne stepped into a shaft of dwindling sunlight, so that her pale skin seemed almost to glow in its whiteness. "Open the gate," she commanded.

Conan watched the guard closely. The man licked lips that seemed to have gone suddenly dry, and made a complex sign in the air with one hand. "Aye," he said, all trace of arrogance suddenly vanished. Whether he recognized Tuanne for what she was or not, he certainly saw *some*thing in her that hurried his wave to the gatetender below. In a moment, the gate swung open with a metal screech.

Inside, Conan's first impressions were mixed: there came to him the city-smells, of people, cooking, and waste, all blended into an aromatic odor unknown outside civilization. A cleared area in front of a row of stone buildings held a man-sized carving of a spider, a hulking monster squatting on eight thick legs. The streets seemed relatively wide, but numerous alleys branched from them, narrow paths between the manmade rock structures.

A small boy stared at the trio, and Conan hailed him.

The boy moved closer. "Are you a barbarian?"

The Cimmerian allowed himself a dry chuckle. "Aye, boy, or so some men name me. But we're looking for someone." He described Skeer, but the boy shook his head. "Hain't seed him. What's that skin you carry?"

"It belonged to a wolf who asked too many questions," Conan said. "Would you know the man we seek if you should see him?"

"Aye, giant sir."

"Good." Conan turned to Elashi. "Do you have any coins?"

"A few."

"Give the boy a copper."

Elashi fished in her pouch and produced a coin. She flipped it toward the boy, who caught it deftly.

Conan said, "Now, boy, if you see this man, come and find me, and there will be two more coppers for you."

"I shall go and look instantly, sir!"

"Nay, hold. How many ways are there out of this city?"

"There are but two, sir. This entrance, and the one which leads to the enclosed valley to the north, where our crops are grown."

"Better. You stay here and watch to see if the man leaves. Direct me to a trader, where I might sell this pelt."

The boy gave Conan a complicated set of turnings, and the big Cimmerian nodded. Leading Elashi and Tuanne, he set off to find the trader's store.

As it turned out, the trader kept his stock mostly outside, under a blue-striped tarp. When Conan strode into the tent without walls, bearing the dire-wolf pelt, a short and thin man seemed to appear from nowhere, to begin clucking over the fur.

"Ah, a fine pelt, fine. Dire-wolf, is it not? Of course, it needs to be properly tanned and the head is missing, so it is less than perfect; still, I might be moved to offer a piece of silver for it, for I am feeling generous today."

Tuanne touched Conan on the shoulder, her fingers chilly against his skin. He turned toward her.

"No less than five silver pieces," she whispered. "White dire-wolves are rare, and he will likely realize twice that much when he sells it."

The merchant was so busy rubbing the fur that he missed the whispered advice. Conan's next words brought him out of his trance.

"Eight pieces of silver," the young Cimmerian said.

The trader looked as if someone had spat upon him.

"Eight? Eight? Are you mad? Has the sun cooked your brain? Even a man as generous as I would be taking bread from the mouths of his children to offer more than three silvers for such a moldy skin!"

Conan allowed himself another small smile. Traders were the same everywhere, it seemed. They would rather bargain than breathe.

Conan shrugged. "I would not wish to be the cause of seeing your children starve. Perhaps I could accept seven and eat less well myself."

The man practically bounced, so much was he enjoying himself. "Four. Four would force me to borrow from my burial money—would you have a man remain above the ground, outlander, for a trifling amount of silver?"

Conan rubbed at his chin. "A serious matter, merchant.

Still, to accept less than six might well cause me the same fate.''

The merchant fingered the pelt, and gave Conan a shrewd appraisal.

Without seeming to, Conan looked around. Several rough-looking men had drifted toward the tent. Three of them bore daggers thrust through their belts, but none carried swords or pikes.

"Your barbarian disguise is very clever," the merchant said, "but it does not fool me. I know a trader when I speak to one. Five, and that is my final offer."

Conan nodded. "You are too sharp for me, master tradesman. I accept."

The little man grinned. He slapped Conan on one hard shoulder, seemed surprised by the muscle there, and nodded.

The exchange proceeded. As the five silver coins flashed in the rapidly fading sunlight, Conan was very much aware of the five men who watched the transaction with more than casual interest. Elashi and Tuanne also seemed to notice the attention. When Elashi made to speak, Conan silenced her with a gesture.

"Ho, master merchant," the Cimmerian said, "that anvil yonder seems to be placed badly."

The merchant nodded. "Aye. My two loutish assistants dragged it there and could move it no further. They have been gathering their strength for several days before attempting to relocate it."

"Where would you have it?"

"There, by the barrel of ironware."

"I shall move it for you."

With that, Conan walked to the large anvil, a chunk of black-painted iron easily equal to his own weight. He squatted, wrapped his fingers around either end, and stood.

With the anvil held to his chest, he turned easily toward the merchant. "It seems that this must be hollow."

"Hollow? Nay, friend, it is solid pig iron, the best casting."

Conan pressed the anvil upward until it was at arm's length over his head. He repeated the motion thrice more before holding the weight as before. "Are you certain? It seems no more than a hollow shell, filled with, say, feathers."

The effect of this demonstration was not lost upon the market riffraff who had been watching. These worthies suddenly recalled that they had business elsewhere, or so it seemed to Conan. He heard small mutterings—

"—by the Nameless, no one is that strong—!"

"—not trifle with that barbarian—"

"—by Set, I'll not risk it—!"

—and the five drifted away as they had come.

Conan carried the anvil to the location indicated by the merchant and set it down as softly as a mother would a sleeping child.

"I would fire both my loutish assistants if you wished work as their replacement."

"Thank you, good merchant, but no. I have five pieces of silver, and therefore do not need to work."

When Conan turned back toward Elashi and Tuanne, he saw that both women were staring at him.

"By Mitra's Left Nostril," Elashi said, "I have never seen a man with your strength! How could you move such a thing so easily?"

Tuanne did not speak, but nodded her agreement with Elashi's question.

Conan felt quite pleased with himself. "That trinket? It was nothing. Come, let us find lodging for the night. In the morning, we shall locate Skeer and make an end to this business.''

When they left the merchant's store, Conan's walk held more than a little swagger. A man could find himself in much worse places than this: to have frightened dangerous men and impressed beautiful women with a single action, and to have silver in one's purse. Yes, there were much worse places for a man to be.

Nine

The guard posted above the South Gate of Opkothard could not recall when he had seen a stranger lot than had come to visit the city. Yesterday, a pilgrim alone who looked more like a footpad than a True Believer had come. Then, a muscle-laden barbarian, bearing a white animal skin and two women, one of whom was obviously a priestess of Him With No Name. The touch of her gaze made him cold, and he was quick to allow them in—he did not need the One With No Name frowning upon him. Then, after the sun went down, six priests had arrived in the darkness, though it was the guard's belief that darkness meant little to them, for they were certainly blind. Never a misstep had one of them made, however, and he also did not doubt that he would walk halfway around the city to avoid meeting these six in any secluded place. And finally, just before his watch was to end, a single robed figure approached.

"Who goes there?" the guard called out.

"I am Malo, priest-initiate of the Suddah Oblates."

The guard knew of that order; they had passed in and

out of the city before. But this one carried a sword in a belt fastened around his waist, and the Suddah had never shown arms before. Still, it was not his job to divine the peculiarities of some minor religion. The Suddah were allowed in, and that was the end of it.

The guard gestured to the gatekeep, and once more, the massive iron slabs forced a protesting groan from the hinges as the gate swung open.

"I feel that which we seek," Tuanne said. "That way." She pointed. Ahead lay a crooked street that wound through a shabbier section of the city. The moon, if it shone, did so behind a thick blanket of clouds, and the only light came from guttering torches set at sparse intervals on poles along the road.

Conan said, "Since Skeer has seen us all, 'twould be best if we caught him unawares. I favor obtaining a meal and room for the night, then rising early."

"That is a good idea," Elashi said. She sounded amazed that any such thought could have come from her companion.

Conan turned toward her, started to speak, then thought better of it. Never mind. It did not matter.

"There is an inn just ahead," Tuanne said.

Conan squinted into the darkness. His eyes, though sharper than most, failed to see sign of an inn.

Tuanne chuckled, the first laugh Elashi and Conan had heard from her. She said, "I am used to the darkness. My sight has had many years to adjust."

She led them down the narrow street, and the smell of something spicy cooking wafted to Conan's nostrils. His mouth watered. Aside from roots, he had eaten nothing for several days. The meat of dire-wolves was sour, according to Tuanne, and the rancid stench of the carcass he had skinned had been enough to convince Conan that it was better left uneaten.

They came to the inn, a stone building with a wooden door and shutters, and a sign hung over the portal. The sign, an unpainted wooden plank, had burned into it the design of a spider. Big on that around here they were, Conan thought. He did not recognize the words etched with some hot tool into the wood under the picture.

"It is called 'The Tarantula,' " Tuanne said.

Elashi shuddered. "I know that name. It is a large spider, big as a man's hand. I have seen them in the desert."

"Poison?" Conan asked.

"No. No more than a bad sting from the bite, so my people say. But hairy and ugly."

Conan dismissed the subject from his thoughts. That a thing might be hairy and ugly worried him not. Poison was another matter.

"Skeer is not within," Tuanne announced. "At least the talisman is not, and I cannot imagine that he would release it from his grasp."

Conan nodded. "Then we shall enter and dine."

Several fat torches lined the walls of the inn, giving everything a smoky, yellow cast. Four men and two women sat or stood about in the central room, eating, talking, or just taking in the warmth of the fire set in the large hearth in one corner. It smelled clean enough.

Tuanne moved to a wooden table near the fire, Elashi and Conan following. The room's occupants cast lazy glances at the trio, but none moved to speak, and none seemed concerned over the visitors.

After a moment, a portly woman wrapped in a stained

lined apron approached. ''What'll be for ye this night, strangers?''

''Wine,'' Conan said, ''and food. Bread, meat, what have you.''

''No meat, I'm afraid, big man. All eaten. I have cheese, sharp and green, bread, black and crusty, and all the wine ye can hold.''

Conan felt a pang of hunger for a seared slab of beef, but he had long ago learned to make do with what was available. ''Aye, mistress innkeep, bring those things, then.''

She waddled away, to return shortly with a platter bearing two loaves of black bread, a head-sized chunk of fragrant cheese, and three brass cups. After a moment, she fetched a pair of wine bottles and set them onto the table. ''Four coppers for the meal,'' she said.

''Have you a room?''

The woman looked shrewdly at Conan, and grinned. ''One room for the three of ye?''

''Aye.''

''To be sure, to be sure. Another four coppers.''

''What is the rate of copper to silver in this town?'' Conan asked.

The woman hesitated for a moment, then grinned. ''No point in trying to fool a man what can take care of two women at once,'' she said. ''Ten to one.''

Automatically, Conan said, ''I had heard fifteen.''

''Well, in some quarters, may be. Here, twelve to one would be more appropriate.''

Conan did not feel like haggling, since the food lay in front of him. He handed the woman one of his silver coins. ''Here, then, for the meal and room, and the balance for your service.''

"Ah, a generous man ye be, young sir." The woman took the coin and walked away.

The bread was not warm, but neither was it stale; the cheese indeed had a hard sharpness, and the wine tasted sweet and dry. Conan ate with gusto, as did Elashi. Tuanne ate nothing, but pretended to sip from her cup and occasionally stirred bits of bread and cheese around the platter for any who might be watching.

After the meal, the three were shown their room, a clean, if small, space up a flight of stairs. There was, however, a slight problem.

"There is only one mat," Elashi said.

"But surely large enough for three," the innkeep said. She flashed a wicked and knowing grin.

"Bring another mat," the desert woman said firmly.

The woman nodded and turned away. Under her breath, but still audible, she muttered, "Trouble in paradise, eh?"

Conan smiled, but wiped the expression away at the sight of Elashi's sudden glare at him.

"I would share your bed, Conan," Tuanne said. "The night is cold, and your warmth appreciated."

Elashi's reaction to this was, as much she had done while with Conan, unexpected. When the portly innkeep returned, dragging a second sleeping mat, the desert woman said to her, "I have changed my mind. It is too cold to sleep alone. I will bed with them." She waved one hand airily at Conan and Tuanne.

The innkeeper's wicked grin returned. "Aye, I have no trouble understanding that."

"We shall only *sleep* together," Elashi said. "For warmth."

"Of course, mistress. Of course."

*   *   *

Skeer fared somewhat less well at that very moment. He had no desire to call attention to himself, and therefore had rented a small sleeping stall in a pigsty of an inn, so that he might be thought poor. He had stretched a line of fishing cord across the entrance to the doorless stall at ankle level. The string, while thin, was sufficiently strong that a man trying to pass through the doorway in the dark would very likely be tripped. Skeer slept with his dagger clutched in one hand, and lightly enough so the thud of a falling body would sure awaken him in time to use the blade before the intruder recovered from his loss of balance. Further, he had taken the precaution of using his dagger to dig a small hole in the dirt under the rancid hay that served for a bed, whereupon he hid the talisman. Buried and the dirt smoothed over, a casual search would not reveal his treasure.

In truth, Skeer did not think he would be bothered during the night. Of the six stalls in the drafty building, none but three was occupied. One contained a drunkard, stinking of sour wine and snoring loudly enough to disturb the dead's slumber; the second held a badly wheezing white-haired man who must have seen seventy winters, all of them hard; and the last cell held himself. While it was unlikely that anyone still followed him, it was even less likely that, should that be the case, they would seek him here. Certainly no one would freely stay here, had he any other choice.

On the morrow, Skeer would seek to replenish his fortunes somewhat, to obtain a horse and supplies, and be off. While he would dally in better quarters and with warmer company than those snoring and wheezing about him at the moment, he would not do so at the expense of his hide. Should Neg discern that one of his agents dared to disobey his orders, said agent's life would be worth less than road dust.

With that pleasant thought echoing in his mind, Skeer slipped into an uneasy sleep.

The Men With No Eyes moved silently through the streets, unhampered by the shroud of night that gave most men pause. The torches flamed low, where they still glowed at all, and the clouds had dropped to become thick fog. The city of Opkothard lay encrusted in swirling cold, the Stygian darkness hiding its secrets from sight—but not from the Men With No Eyes. They moved as one, checking for any sign of the zombie Tuanne. Though blind, their ears caught the faintest sounds; the footsteps of a rat in an alley thundered in their ears. Though blind, their nostrils could scent the sweet smell of a man with a woman, behind closed doors. Though blind, their skins caught the faint heat of an old man smoking a pipe as he lay sleepless in his bed, remembering his past days of youth and glory. Lack of sight meant little to these evil priests, and they moved almost tirelessly, predators on the hunt. They would find that which they sought, or they would not return to their temple.

They would find her.

Malo settled in a wool-shed, burrowing among the bales of fleece for warmth. His questions had determined that the barbarian who had slain two of his brother priests had indeed sought refuge here. Well, he would not find it.

That the one who called himself Conan had killed Cengh and Mikahl the Messenger Malo doubted not at all. The evidence was indisputable. The barbarian lout had fled, taking with him the Source of Light which the messenger had brought to the temple. Would an innocent man flee? Surely not.

That the Cimmerian ape had humbled and embarrassed Malo in front of his teacher merely added fuel to Malo's righteous anger. He had been quick to volunteer to join the searchers for the slayer of the two Oblates. Only this time, there would be no *fimbo* rules to observe. The blade Malo now had lying next to his hand was of fine Turanian steel, folded many times during its forging for strength, with an edge he could use to shave his beard. Let the ape try to catch it in his hand as he had the wooden blade, and it would be blood and bones in the dirt of the street!

For the deaths of the Oblates, Conan must die. For the embarrassment of Malo, that death would be slow and painful. He would carve the barbarian like a straw practice-post, filling the gutters with the pieces!

On the morrow he would find the killer. On the morrow, the killer would pay. With that thought, Malo slipped into a sleep laced with glorious and bloody dreams.

In the heart of Opkothard, in the depths of a black temple dedicated to the Eight-Legged God With No Name, a rail-thin priest tended to his obscene ministrations. On the altar lay the entrails of a fresh-killed ram. A dozen black spiders, each with a belly bearing a red hourglass design, scuttled through the gore. The priest watched the patterns created by the spiders, and his divinations filled him with worry. There were dangerous men in the city, some bearing Powers better not trifled with, some seeking those energies. Such men as these could create many problems, if proper attention were not paid.

The thin priest watched the spiders a moment longer, then reached for the ceremonial club at his belt. The spiders, having served their one-time purpose, were no longer energized. Carefully, but with the proper detachment, the priest smashed each of the spiders into pulp. They were all female, the spiders, and what he did to them was no more than they did to their mates, once the males had served their purpose. The wheel spun, as always, completing the cosmic cycle.

The results of this divination must be taken at once to Emreaves, the High Priest. He might wish to take steps against these intruders into the sanctity of the spider-god's mountain stronghold.

One of the spiders trembled on the altar, probably no more than a nervous spasm, but the priest paused and brought the ceremonial club down upon it with great force. Parts of gut splattered, and the gory effluvia stained his robe, but he took no notice of it. The ceremony was the important thing; a robe could be washed, but a haunting by an ill-used spider was another thing altogether.

Ten

Skeer awoke to the muffled sound of a man yelling nearby; in fact, the man making the racket lay sprawled upon the floor of Skeer's unkempt sleeping stall, more or less face-down in the filthy hay. This posture was responsible for the reduced volume of the man's cry, it being difficult to make much noise with a mouthful of compost.

The thief came up from sleep all of a moment. He rolled from his pallet toward the intruder, the point of his knife leading. It was but a second's work for Skeer to grab the fallen man's hair and pull his head back to expose the throat. He laid the edge of his blade against the strangely clean skin. By the thin shaft of morning sun that penetrated the stall through a warped board, Skeer took stock. He recognized the man as the drunk who had occupied one of the other sleeping stalls earlier. The artfully tied fishing line had not failed in its purpose. Now, what was the man about?

Skeer posed the question. "What are you doing in here?"

The odor of the sour wine nauseated him when the man

99

opened his mouth to reply. "Ah, ah, ah, good sir, my lord, I—I, I 'uz just lookin' for—for—"

"Come on, man, spit it out!"

An unfortunate choice of words, it seemed. The drunk started to heave; his mouth opened, and a torrent of stinking liquid gushed forth.

"By Set!" Skeer leaped backward to avoid the rush of vomitus as the drunk continued heaving.

After a moment, the stench in the fetid cell rose to fill every corner, it seemed. Skeer's own belly rumbled at the high odor.

The drunk, smiling, said, "I 'uz in search of the night stall, my lord. Nature called."

"Out!" Skeer yelled. "And mind the line!"

The drunk managed to raise himself to a wobbly stance, and, despite Skeer's warning, tripped over the string across the doorway as he exited. After a moment, he shambled off down the hallway.

Wonderful, Skeer thought. Such a place is this that a drunk mistakes my sleeping room for an outhouse! It was past time to be away from here, of that there was no doubt.

Quickly, Neg's agent went to dig up his treasure.

As Skeer departed from his ill-spent night lodging, an unseen figure stood in the shadows, watching intently. Skeer rounded a corner, out of sight, and the watcher moved into the light, revealing the drunken man who had recently lain upon the floor of Skeer's quarters. Now, however, the man's gaze seemed sharp and unfogged by wine; and, when he moved, his gait revealed only steadiness, with no trace of alcoholic crippling.

The drunk smiled.

A second figure slipped from the shadows, to stand near the drunk. This proved to be the old man who had also occupied a stall in Skeer's most recent quarters. His white hair was no less so, but his manner betrayed the color, as he moved more like a man in his summer than in his winter.

"Get to the High Priest," the ersatz drunk said to the facsimile of an old man. "Tell him I am certain this is the outlander he seeks. He is much too alert for a man with nothing to hide."

"Emreaves will be pleased to hear of this," the other said.

"Go, then. The faster you bespeak it to him, the quicker he will be pleased."

"By your command, Disguise Master. May the Nameless One be with you."

"He can be anywhere he pleases, as long as his priests continue to pay so well."

The High Priest of the Opkothardian Temple of the Spider God With No Name nodded at the message delivered by the man decorated with the skill of the Disguise Master's art. That the man was little more than a novitiate priest, carrying twenty-odd winters, could not be determined from his appearance.

The Disguise Master, while not a True Believer, had his uses. This instance proved to be one of them. Although the message from his Under Priest had only confirmed that which Emreaves had already felt, the exact identity of the man bearing the power-emanating talisman had been less than clear. It was here and someone bore it, that much had been certain; more than that he could only guess at, and such a thing was much too dangerous to risk by mere guessing. He must *know*, and he must act upon that

knowledge before the magical device might be used. The
One With No Name frowned upon stray magics in his
domain, and it fell to his priests to prevent such powers
from coming to fruition.

Emreaves said, "Good. Return and find the Disguise
Master. Do as he commands, and bid him to continue his
surveillance upon this outlander until I contact him."

The young priest bowed. "My lord."

After the young-man-disguised-as-an-old-one departed,
Emreaves left the antechamber and moved to the inner
sanctum. There were prayers to be mounted and rituals to
be observed, after which he could strike the bearer of the
magical device with karmic impunity. It remained only to
determine the manner of the outlander's demise, and there
would be little difficulty in that: he had so many methods
from which to choose. . . .

Conan awoke from a dream in which he had lain with
two women, neither of whom could get enough of him. As
his eyes caught the faint gleam of morning's first light into
the room, he realized that he did indeed lie between two
women, and he smiled.

"Pleasant thoughts?" asked Tuanne.

Conan said, "You awaken early."

"I do not sleep in the manner of normal women," she
said. "But I thank you for your warmth in the night."

"Gladly given."

To his opposite side, Elashi stirred. For a brief moment,
she pressed her full breasts against Conan and draped one
leg over his hips. "Mmm," she said. Then, she opened
her eyes, stiffened, and quickly pulled away from contact
with the big Cimmerian.

"Let us go and find Skeer," Conan said, before Elashi could speak.

"Yes," she said, "we should do that."

Five of the Men With No Eyes stood outside the Tarantula Inn in their dark robes, unspeaking and unmoving. The morning's chill seemed not to bother them, and their breathing made steam-fog in slow and steady patterns. After a moment, the sixth priest emerged from the inn and nodded to the others. Two of the priests moved to cover the inn's front entrance, while two others circled around the back to take up positions behind the back exit. The final two priests reentered the inn. Without pause, they began to ascend the stairs toward the sleeping rooms.

Malo had wasted no time in his search for the barbarian killer. Before first light, he had arisen from his bed of musty wool and begun looking for night workers. He found several: garbage haulers, trulls, and those with insomnia. While Opkothard was a large city, it was not so large that the passage of strangers went unnoticed. Before an hour had passed, Malo knew that a larger barbarian had spent the night in a local inn, accompanied by two women.

Malo spat when he heard this. The man was no doubt spending some ill-gotten loot on painted whores, while laughing over the slaying of two priests. Well. He would laugh no more when Malo finished with him.

Skeer had spotted a likely horse to steal, along with a shop that could supply food and blankets for the remainder of his trip. He need only fetch the supplies—the shop's owner had thoughtfully inscribed his arrival time at his place of business upon the doorjamb, and it would be an

hour hence—and be off. By the time anyone knew anything was missing, Skeer the wily would be a long way
down the road.

He was just making ready to enter the shop when he felt
a sense of being watched.

Skeer had no magical talents, depending instead on his
skills for survival; still, this particular sense had saved him
more than once, and he was loath to distrust it. Without
being obvious, Neg's agent checked his surroundings.

At first, he saw no one. But after a second scan, he
spotted the worker. The man seemed to take no notice of
Skeer, engrossed as he was in loading manure from a large
mound of the same substance into a rude wooden pull-cart.
Industriously, the man shoveled, pausing only to wipe his
brow on one dirty sleeve.

Skeer considered his position. True, the manurist could
see him, but certainly seemed to have no interest other
than his labor; and the man had nothing of the familiar
about him—Skeer deemed it certain he had never seen him
before; still, that crawly feeling persisted. Perhaps there
existed some unseen watcher, peering from behind a blind
or curtain. Perhaps even some magical ward protected the
shop's interior?

Skeer shook his head. No, this no longer seemed such
an easy victory. He decided to seek another target.

He walked away from the shop front, past the manure
loader, who never looked up at him.

You seek shadows where none exist, Skeer told himself.
But he did not turn back toward the shop.

Conan had just buckled his sword sheath around his
waist when the door to the room burst inward and slammed

against the wall. Two men stepped inside and looked directly at Tuanne.

At least they pointed their noses in her direction. For Conan could see that their eyes held only blank grayness where other men had pupils.

Tuanne's reaction consisted of a catlike hiss. She backed up two steps, until her back met the wall and she could go no farther.

Conan said, "Tuanne?"

"Neg's men," she said, "come for me! They are called Men With No Eyes."

Conan's sword sang its song of steel and leather as he whipped the blade free of its sheath. "They will soon be called the men with no heads, do they not depart!"

The two men turned to face the Cimmerian.

"They are dangerous, Conan! Deadly!"

"They are not even armed," Conan observed aloud.

"There is no need. They are skilled and abnormally strong!"

"We shall see how skilled and strong they are. You," he said to the priests, "leave my room, now!"

The men moved away from each other, as if to encircle Conan.

The Cimmerian youth gripped his sword in both hands, fingers loose, and aimed the point of his weapon at the chest of the nearer man.

To Conan's left, Elashi drew her blade and turned so she covered his left side. To his right, Tuanne picked up the earthen water pitcher and held it over her head, as if to throw it. Conan grinned. By Crom, to have two women who would *fight* . . . Well, a man could hardly do better!

The first priest moved, and his speed surprised Conan. He leaped in, kicked at Conan's knee, and leaped back, all before the muscular Cimmerian could swing his blade. He did manage to shift his leg, so that the knee-strike only thudded against a thick thigh instead. Even so, the force of the kick shoved Conan half a foot backward.

So. Tuanne's assessment of the men had not been in error. They were both fast and strong. Then again, Conan was no weakling.

"Haah!" the Cimmerian screamed and charged, blade cocked over his shoulder.

Fast he might be, and strong, but the attacker had only as much space to maneuver as the room allowed, and it allowed little. When he would have danced lithely backward, the wall refused him passage. Conan's blade came down, set to shear the man open from skull to crotch.

Amazingly, the blind man twisted to one side. He was good. But not good enough to avoid the sword's edge entirely. Sharpened iron met the flesh of his arm, and the sword hardly paused in its passage. The arm flew from its owner.

He was not done, this one-armed one. He spun in a short circle and thrust out his bare heel. The kick caught Conan in the pit of the belly and knocked him backward.

"Oof!"

Though corded with muscle, the strike still hurt Conan's midsection enough to draw from him the expletive.

The priest made an error then, by trying to follow up. Conan was not injured greatly, and when the Man With No Eyes leaped in, swinging his remaining arm, he was skewered like a bird on a spit. Even in death he made no sound, as he sagged.

The second attacker, busy trying to grab Tuanne, had troubles of his own. First, the zombie woman tossed the water pitcher at him. When he raised his arm to ward it off, Elashi darted under his guard and sliced across his ribs with her sword. It was not a deadly cut, but it was messy; blood welled and spattered as he leaped backward.

Before the man could recover, both Conan and Elashi moved in, thrusting with their blades almost in unison. Conan's stab took the man in the throat, Elashi's in the belly. He fell, mortally injured.

"So much for them," Conan said.

"There will be others," Tuanne said, out of breath. "Neg would never send just two. We must leave quickly!"

Aye, Conan would favor that. These two had been much too quick to suit him.

They started down the stairs.

Malo arrived at the inn bearing the likeness of a spider on its front. A pair of men stood to the sides of the door, watching intently. At least it seemed that way, until he got closer. He shuddered. Unlikely they watched anything with *those* eyes!

But his quarry lay within, and he was in no mood to be delayed.

"Ho, friends. I would enter the inn."

The two men turned as one to stare sightlessly at him.

Hmm. Perhaps it would be better to wait for the barbarian to exit . . . ?

Less than three heartbeats later, the barbarian did so, at a run. As fast as the two door-watchers moved, Conan was past them before they could react. More, the damned barbarian had with him the women of whom Malo had heard.

The Suddah Oblate reached for his sword.

His muscles warmed by his earlier exertions, Conan's

reactions now were speeded up. He whipped his sword around in a short arc in time to catch the lunging blind attacker squarely on top of the head.

It truly was a fine blade, Conan thought, as the flesh and bone bisected neatly.

The second blind one gave out a piercing whistle, and Conan's instant feeling was that the sound was a signal. Best they depart, quickly!

He turned toward the whistler and began swinging his sword back and forth in snappy cuts, moving forward. "Stay behind me," he commanded Elashi and Tuanne.

The attacker had no choice but to give ground, and he did so as Conan wove a path away from the inn.

Malo moved for Conan. Just then, two more of the strange-eyed men stormed around the side of the inn. They became aware of Malo, and mistakenly thought him an enemy, for they moved toward him.

Malo bore these two no ill will; however, their intent seemed plain enough, and he raised his Turanian steel in a defensive pose. "You are mistaken," he said. "I am not with them."

His words seemed to have no effect. One of the men darted toward him, and Malo's automatic reaction was to flick a cut at him. It cost the attacker the better part of his left hand. Malo grinned. This was his first real fight in ten years of training. If these men would take him, why, let them try! He would finish the barbarian later. He shuffled his feet, right, left, right, left, in the economical slide steps he had been taught. Warily, the two blind men moved back.

Skeer heard the fight before he saw it. His inclination

was to turn and move the other way, opposite the crowd that appeared from nowhere as they always seemed to do when a fight broke out. But the best way to blend in was to go with the flow, so he circled a horse stall with the others to see the cause of the outcry.

What he observed sent very cold chills rolling along over his spine, and forced a sweat onto his brow.

By Set! It was that barbarian lout from the temple! And the zombie bitch was with him! More, one of the Suddah Oblates also waved a sword in the air, and four—no, three of the Men With No eyes opposed them—one seemed to be very dead, and one of the remaining ones bled rather profusely. And there was a girl he did not know, also engaging in swordplay.

Something was wrong here.

Skeer did not understand all that he observed, but he understood that none of it was to his benefit. The barbarian and the zombie were bad enough; that Neg had sent some of his damned priests also did not bode well.

His first reaction was to flee—to grab the nearest horse and ride for the South Gate at a full gallop. But even as he watched the barbarian cut down another of the priests, Skeer's sense of caution took him. He had a vision of himself being stopped at the gate by some unknown agent, tugged from his stolen mount, and enchained. The vision filled him, leaving no room for doubt. That it could happen seemed quite likely, what with all *this* going on. What else might be possible? No, he would hide in the city until darkness, and utilize stealth for his escape.

With the clash of steel in his ears, Skeer hurried away from the battle.

"It is him!" Tuanne yelled.

Conan, busy chopping at one of the priests, did not register the exclamation's meaning.

"What? Who is it?"

"Skeer. And he's getting away!"

The big Cimmerian managed to cut down his opponent just then, when the man slipped on something in the street and half-fell. Conan assisted his meeting with the dirt.

Behind him, another priest toppled, headless. This one was attacked by someone Conan did not recognize at first. After a moment, he recalled the face: Malo, the priest he had sparred with at the Oblates' temple. Good that he chose now to appear, Conan thought.

Elashi, though spirited, lacked both strength and speed to match her opponent. Tuanne, however, was assisting the desert woman, and between the two of them, they managed to keep the last blind man at bay.

Conan stepped in behind the man. "Ho!" he said.

The man turned at this new threat, and Conan drove his sword's point through the man's breastbone and heart.

Even as the priest fell, Tuanne called out. "Hurry, Skeer escapes!"

But as Conan and the two women turned to leave, they found their path blocked—by Malo.

"Stand aside, priest!" Conan commanded. "A murderer makes good his escape."

"Aye," Malo said, "perhaps. But another shall not!"

"Are you daft? There are no murderers here! We fought to protect ourselves!"

"Your tongue should freeze from your lies," Malo said. He raised his sword over his head, edge up, and angled so that it formed a horizontal shield. "This blade is not wood, barbarian, and neither do you wear a gauntlet."

"Conan!" Tuanne cried. "Skeer moves farther away."

"I have not the time for this, Malo! Move!"

"To examine your corpse I shall move."

Conan's rage rose to fill him. He lifted his heavy sword high, as a man preparing to split firewood might, and leaped.

Malo held his position, sword raised to block. His form was perfect.

Unfortunately, Malo's training had not prepared him for the wrath of Conan of Cimmeria. Conan's blued iron weapon came down so fast and hard that it whistled in the morning air. The force of the blow knocked Malo's blade down, and the brawny Cimmerian's razored edge bit into Malo's forehead, slicing him open as might a cook opening a melon.

The spirit of Malo, Suddah Oblate, escaped through the rent and went to join his ancestors. By the time the body collapsed to the ground, Malo was quite dead.

Conan, however, did not pause to examine the corpse. He and Tuanne and Elashi left abruptly, chasing the vanished Skeer.

Eleven

During the balance of the day Skeer did not stop for more than a few moments. He snatched a meal almost literally on the run; he felt the urge to keep moving, as if the breath of doom beat hot upon his neck. It seemed more than coincidental that the barbarian and zombie bitch had followed him here; too, the presence of the Men With No Eyes bothered him. And there was something else, some unnamed fear that lurked about him, as if nothing evil dogged his footsteps. This latter fright had no reasonable basis, for he had neither seen nor heard anything to cause it. And yet there was no denying that he felt it. So he moved, casually for the most part, but frequently and without tarrying. To a watcher, he would have seemed unhurried, for he took pains to make it appear so. But to himself, Skeer was in full flight, death pounding along behind him.

"Which way?" Conan asked.

Tuanne closed her eyes, tilted her head slightly backward, then pointed down a twisted street. "There."

Elashi started to run down the street, but Conan caught her arm. "Nay, hold a moment."

Tuanne opened her eyes. "Why do you hesitate?"

The three of them stood at the conflux of four streets, surrounded by more of the ubiquitous stone housery. A wagon of melons sat broiling in the high afternoon sun nearby, giving the air a sickly sweet scent; women picked over the fruit, bargaining with the wagon's owner. Behind Conan, an old man sat by a large water pipe, smoking some aromatic mixture that stained the space around him with blue fumes.

"We have passed this place before," Conan said.

"So?" Elashi made as if to hurry off again.

"We have passed this place and several others more than once. Our quarry is not standing still."

"As always, you state the obvious," Elashi said.

Tuanne raised a hand and touched the other women on the shoulder. "Wait. I think I take his meaning. Skeer is running, and with only my link to the talisman to go on, we cannot follow fast enough to catch him. Is this correct, Conan?"

"Aye."

"Then what would you have us do?" Elashi asked.

"There is only one way out of the city," the Cimmerian said. "Unless he chooses to escape into a box canyon, he must pass through the South Gate. We take up a stance nearby and wait."

"How long?" Elashi said.

"As long as it takes. We can sleep in turns, if need be."

Elashi nodded. "I must admit your plan sounds valid."

Conan wondered why it pained her so to admit such a thing, but he did not speak his thought aloud.

*   *   *

As the barbarian and two women moved off, the old man drawing upon the water pipe stood and abandoned his smoky pleasure. He moved out into the street, to watch the trio. When they were nearly out of sight, he waved. One of the women picking at the melons nodded and hurried off down the street, following the three outlanders. The man selling the melons left his work and scurried over toward the old man.

The smoker wiped at his face, and streaks appeared as the paint-and-powder disguise he wore rubbed off. "These three have something to do with the other one," he said. "Tell the High Priest that I would have another five of his men. Send two of them to the South Gate, and have the other three meet me here. My own agents will continue to follow our quarry."

"By your leave, Disguise Master."

"I have just given it, fool. Go."

In the Inner Sanctum of the temple, Emreaves finished his final ritual. He had only to burn the ceremonial incense for the final touch, and he could safely instigate the Death of the Shes. Not a pleasant way to die, if there was any such method, but a certain one. In the history of the temple, no man had ever lived through the curse of the Shes; indeed, it might not always befall the victim instantly, like a clean lightning bolt, but eventually, befall him it would. The Shes, once summoned, never stopped until they had accomplished their task. For those so condemned who were True Believers, a requisite part of the torture was to inform them of the curse, then do nothing to hinder their escape. Many chose suicide rather than face what would happen in its stead.

Night began to shade the streets outside as Emreaves lit

the ceremonial incense. Pungent smoke wafted into the dark timbers arched over his head, and in the falling light, he imagined he could hear the rustlings of ten thousand tiny feet as they stirred into life.

The High Priest smiled as he waved the incense. Those who carried magic into his city did so at their peril. The Priests of the Nameless would ever see to that.

When evening cast its dark net over the city, Skeer felt much relieved. Darkness was his brother, cloaking the activities of thieves and whores with welcome cover. No one could catch what they could not see, and in the night, Skeer moved among the shadows as one rendered invisible.

Through the day he had not been troubled by the barbarian and his women; neither had he gazed upon any other danger to himself. That bothersome worry persisted, but no manifestation of it had come to pass.

Well. Soon he would be shut of Opkothard and all its problems.

The plan he had mentally drawn was simple: here squatted another of the public inns, replete with a good crowd of wine swillers. Outside, tethered to a rail, a half-dozen horses awaited riders. A sleepy-looking guard leaned against a nearby wall, ostensibly watching the mounts and securing the peace. Skeer would slit the guard's throat, take the strongest-looking mount, and make his way to the gate, wearing the dead man's clothes. If any man searched for him, they would not see anyone in Skeer's raiment approach the exit. He would talk his way past the gatemaster and be off. With the supplies he had liberated a few moments earlier, he could be halfway to Neg's stronghold before he needed to stop; by then, no one could catch him even if they knew where he was bound.

That the barbarian knew Skeer's destination seemed apparent. He was in league with the zombie bitch—he should have severed her head and tossed it far from her body when he'd had the chance, dammit!—and doubtless she had told him of her encounter with Skeer. He berated himself once again for failing to recognize the zombie when first he had seen her. Fool!

Well, there was nothing to be done for it now. Better to accept the past and get on with the present.

The guard nodded, asleep on his feet. Without the wall to prop him, he surely would have fallen. Skeer had no trouble at all walking right up to the doomed man. His greatest worry was how best to dispatch the man without getting blood on the guard's clothing. After a moment of thought, he had the method.

With his knife, Skeer pried a loose paving stone from the road. He hefted it, to get the feel, then drew his arm back and smashed the stone into the guard's temple. He felt the bone give under the blow, and the man fell, instantly unconscious. Likely to die from the cracked skull, given a chance, but Skeer would not risk that. After hurriedly stripping the man of his clothing, Skeer bent and nicked the great vessels on both sides of the unconscious man's neck. As the man's life poured onto the street, Skeer dressed himself in the guard's uniform. In another moment, he had picked a large gray stallion, mounted the low saddle, and urged the horse into a walk. Rot in Gehanna, Opkothard, he thought, as he moved toward the South Gate.

When he stopped at a narrow intersection, to peer around for any sign of pursuit, Skeer thought he heard something. Like tiny fingers tapping lightly on dry paper, it sounded, or rats' feet over broken glass in some dead cellar, perhaps.

Ah, well. It was nothing to worry about. He kicked the horse lightly, and started off.

As the moon sailed across the clear skies dotted with the cold fire of ten thousand stars, Conan shifted uncomfortably upon the edge of the hay cart parked near the South Gate. Though it had been his idea to watch the gate for Skeer's departure, he much disliked the idea of waiting instead of acting. He turned and looked at the two women behind him, lying in the hay. Elashi slept, wrapped in a blanket Conan had found hanging on a line to dry earlier in the day. Tuanne's eyes were open, but she stared sightlessly into space, seeming to take no notice of her surroundings.

The cart had been parked near the juncture of an alley and the main street of Opkothard. From Conan's position, he could easily see the gate, though the shadows of the buildings flanking the alley hid him from all but the sharpest of views.

So it was that when the rider approached, the sharp-eared Cimmerian heard and saw him without being detected by the horseman. One of the nightwatchmen, Conan noted, probably come to relieve the gate guard.

The new guard reined his horse to a halt and called out something to the man posted over the gate. Conan could not quite make out the words, but it seemed that his first idea had been incorrect.

Abruptly, Tuanne sat up, shaking the cart. Conan turned toward her.

"The talisman! It is very near!"

Conan turned back to stare at the new guard. The sliver of moon did not cast enough light to reveal the man's face, but Conan's thoughts leaped ahead of his sight. Though not civilized, his wits were not dull—Skeer sat astride that horse, in disguise.

Drawing his sword, the young giant pushed nimbly away from the cart and started toward the gate.

"Why would ye be desiring exit at this time o' the eve, fellow guildsman?"

Skeer regarded the man with what he hoped was an expression of exasperation. He shrugged. "*I* would not, brother. Hit's the orders of the Watch Commander. He's expecting somebody and I be sent to meet him."

"Why was not I told of this order?"

"Ask the Unnamed One, brother, for I do not know. I just follow orders. Open the gate, hey? and we can discuss the philosophy of upranks when I return."

The gate guard grumbled, muttering some not-quite-beneath-his-breath curse, and finally called down to the gatemaster to crank open the door.

Skeer grinned. This was too easy, fooling fools.

That sound he had heard earlier, the skritch-skritch, suddenly returned. He turned in the saddle and looked behind him. Nothing there—wait! There was a man stalking across the road, a big-shouldered figure whose face was in shadow, but who carried a bared sword in his right hand, and from his size, could be only the barbarian!

He would have tried to hurry the gatemaster, but then Skeer saw something even more riveting than the barbarian: the statue of the spider seemed to be . . . undulating. Skeer strained his eyes against the darkness, and it seemed to him that a living carpet had somehow overlain the stone statue, a dark stain that seemed to ooze down and onto the road. As he watched, the stain moved closer, filling the street. It took a moment for him to see that of which the carpet was actually composed—

Spiders! Thousands of them! They were hairy-legged and big, each at least the size of a man's hand and fingers, all scuttling directly toward the gate!

And directly toward Skeer.

Of a moment, Skeer knew that the arachnids were meant for him. That sense of foreboding he had felt all day focused, and he knew, he *knew* that these hellish creatures sought Skeer and none other.

The thought filled him with terror.

The gate was partially open now, almost wide enough to admit a horseman. Skeer could not wait. He spurred the horse, and the beast leaped forward, knocking the gatemaster sprawling and cursing. Skeer's left knee scraped against the rusty iron and tore his pants leg, but that didn't matter. A bruised knee would heal; the bites of a thousand giant spiders very likely would not.

The guard suddenly caught sight of the advancing tide of eight-legged creatures.

"By the Nameless! Let it not be me!"

He grabbed a torch from its holder and extended it toward the spiders. Yellow light danced over the cobblestones—

Yellow light danced over the cobblestones, and Conan stopped, hearing the guard's yell at the same instant he became aware of the ten thousand tiny footfalls. He looked down, and saw the spiders then, advancing like a wave along a shoreline.

"Crom!"

He would have run, but the first of the hirsute things began to stream past him then, and he might as well have been a tree for all the attention they paid him. The spiders flowed over his feet and around his ankles, but they did not molest him, neither did they pause. Conan stood very still; to step on one might raise the attention of the others, and a sword seemed little defense against such a horde of fat-bodied crawlers.

Skeer, meanwhile, had bolted through the partially opened gate. Conan heard the hoofbeats rapidly gaining away from the city. Damnation! He had escaped again.

He turned and beheld both Elashi and Tuanne, watching in wide-mouthed horror as the street seemed to move under him. Conan breathed very slowly, holding himself as still as he could. If the spiders decided to attack him now, he would be hard-pressed to escape. Elashi had said that these creatures—if they were indeed the same kind whose image decorated the Tarantula Inn—carried no lethal poison. Still, a hundred bites would no doubt carry a man a long way toward meeting his god, and Conan had no desire to join Crom just yet.

It seemed hours, but more likely was no more than a few minutes before the final spiders straggled past him. By this point, the vanguard of the black wave had passed through the open gate. When the last ones had cleared the portal, Conan ran to the city's exit and stared after the retreating mass of eight-legged creatures.

Above him, the guard chanted some prayer over and over; of the gatemaster, there was nothing to be seen. And as for Skeer, he was lost in the distant darkness.

The big Cimmerian looked up at the frightened guard. "What manner of infestation is this?" he called.

"Hail O Nameless and protect thy faithful servant from harm. Hail O Nameless and protect thy faithful servant—"

Conan rapped on the gate with the pommel of his sword. "Guard! Must I scale the wall and separate you from your head? What of the spiders?"

The guard seemed to awaken from a trance. "What?"

"The spiders, the spiders!"

"They are sent by the One With No Name, whose form they copy. It is the Curse of the Shes—each one is female—and they seek the death of one who would oppose the spider-god."

"And who might that be?"

"The guard—the one who left. He must have offended the god."

"Aye, likely he offended more than one god," Conan said. "And escaped, to boot."

The guard looked grave. "Nay, friend. There is no escape from the Shes. If you bear the curse, they will follow ye to the ends of the Earth. They never quit until they accomplish their mission." He shuddered. "I would not be in that man's boots for all the gold in the city."

Conan turned away and walked back to the two women. "We shall have to find horses and supplies," he said. "It seems that Skeer has escaped us once again."

Elashi made as if to speak, then apparently thought better of it. Good. Conan's mood would not have suffered any snideness readily.

Twelve

Conan had four pieces of silver left from his sale of the dire-wolf's skin, but in this city, he could at most buy a single horse for that, and not one apt to carry a man very far before collapsing of old age or infirmity. He needed two horses, at the very least, and three would be better. In addition, he needed supplies, food for two, and assorted gear for travel—blankets, cooking utensils, and the like. They had not the time to earn these things, for every hour that passed gave Skeer that much more of a lead.

So it would be theft that gave them what they needed, Conan reasoned. There were many men who had much more than necessary for comfort, and the Cimmerian had no qualms about taking from the rich. As a boy, he had gone with other men on raids from Cimmeria; booty from these raids was considered just compensation. In this case it would not be war, but certainly it was necessary.

Men in cities tended to keep their gold and silver either well-hidden or well-protected, or both, and so the theft of money might entail no small risk. Thievery being a skill he had only the rudiments of, Conan felt no great confidence in his ability without more practice. If he had to go directly to the items he needed, however, it meant also no small amount of time used to locate mounts and supplies, and then to liberate them. Time was the key factor here: with each passing moment Skeer distanced himself farther. So, the trick lay in minimizing the risk but gaining hard currency as soon as possible.

It came at this point that the Cimmerian noted something rather strange: a night workman stretching canvas for an awning nearby. Not that there was anything strange about the man or his actions per se, but rather in the manner—there was something passing familiar in his motions.

As Conan watched the man, it came to him. Early in the day, he had passed an old man smoking from a water pipe. Something about the set of this man's moves brought that old man to mind. They looked nothing alike, the two, and yet, bodies did not lie as did clothing. He was reminded of Skeer, posing as a guard just an hour past.

Conan, Elashi, and Tuanne walked past the man, and the worker gave no obvious indication that he watched them. And yet, now that the thought lodged in his mind, the young Cimmerian felt an interest from the man, almost as a pressure upon his back. What could it mean?

Conan grinned.

"Something is amusing?" Elashi asked.

"Aye. Perhaps."

The Disguise Master waited until the trio was out of sight, then he abandoned the awning and hurried to circle the block of housing and stables, to await further sight of the barbarian and two women. As he ran, he shed his outer layer of clothing, to reveal a long robe that had been carefully rolled up around his waist. With motions made economical through practice, he shook the robe loose, raised the cowl that had been hidden under his jacket, and lo! he was no longer a worker, but a priest.

He slid to a stop well ahead of the trio he followed. From beneath the robe, he pulled a prayer mat, and quickly unrolled it and laid it upon the door stoop of a small temple dedicated to the worship of Vela, a minor harvest deity. He knelt upon the mat, pressed his hands together in prayer, and lifted his eyes to stare toward the night sky.

He heard the voices, then the footsteps, as his quarry approached. Ah, yes, he could see them peripherally—but wait—there were only two, the women. Where was the giant outlander—?

Night-cooled metal touched the Disguise Master's throat at that moment, and he instantly knew to where exactly the barbarian had gotten.

"Why do you spy on us?" Conan asked.

"M-m-my son, you are mistaken—"

Conan tossed the clothes he had seen the man strip away moments earlier in front of the "priest."

The man swallowed. "W-what do you want of me?"

"Answer my question."

"I am paid by the High Priest of the Nameless One. I followed the one who left the city pursued by the curse of the spiders."

"Then why watch us? He is no friend of ours."

"You came together; you pursued him; there is a link. The High Priest will have no mystery in his city."

"Ah. And were you well paid for this labor?"

When the man spoke, pride tinged his voice. "Yes. I

am the best in this city at what I do. My disguises are second to none, and I am never seen.''

''Until now. I hope you have some of this pay upon your person.''

''Why?''

''As a token of your affection. And to maintain the integrity of your neck.'' Conan pressed the sword a bit deeper into the spy's throat.

''In my purse,'' the man said. His voice now seemed little more than a whisper.

Elashi and Tuanne had come to stand in front of Conan and his captured footpad-spy. Conan said, ''Fetch his purse.''

Elashi bent and pulled open the leather pouch on the man's belt.

''Mitra! He carries gold! A dozen coins, at least!''

To the spy Conan said, ''Well paid, indeed. And what measure of affection would you have us take as compensation for being the first to penetrate your skills?''

''A-a-all of it.''

The big Cimmerian withdrew his sword's pressure against the man's flesh, grinning as he did so. ''Nay, we would not leave a man without a copper. What price would it take to buy three horses and supplies for a month's travel?''

''Two gold solons.''

''Take three,'' Conan ordered Elashi.

''Only three? But surely a man who carries this much on his person must have much more buried somewhere—''

''Nay, three is all we need.''

''You are generous,'' the spy said. ''I have no argument with you. I will be on my way—''

''Hold,'' Conan said, lifting the sword to point at the spy's belly. ''I would rather you did not run to your High Priest until we are well away from this city.''

"I would not think of it—"

"And to that end, I think we should bind you."

"It is not necessary. I shall give you my oath—"

"My experience is that rope binds better than oaths," Conan said. "Or, in this case, strips from the clothing you abandoned should do."

"Truly you need not do this," the spy began.

Elashi leaned over and said, "Better bound than to have one's throat slit, eh? My friend over there loves to watch blood flow. Sometimes he drinks it."

The spy shuddered, cast a fearful glance at Conan, and quickly extended his hands, wrists crossed, to be bound.

Moments later, the trio headed for the trader's store where Conan had sold the dire-wolf's pelt only little more than a day past.

"I am certain he would not mind doing business with us, even at this late hour, if we obtain two gold coins worth of good but pay him three."

"Then we leave this night?" Elashi said.

"The road is visible, and if Skeer travels in the dark, so can we," Conan replied. "At least far enough away so that casual pursuit will not happen upon us."

"Travel at night is not so bad," Tuanne said. "One can get used to it."

They continued to the merchant's place.

Neg stood contemplating his image in the looking glass when one of the Men With No Eyes glided silently into view behind him. The necromancer turned. "Yes?"

They did not speak, these blind priests, but they had a rich vocabulary of gestures and signs. The priest held up six fingers, pointed to himself, then drew a finger across his throat sharply. The message could be no plainer.

"Dead? All six?"

The priest nodded.

"Set curse them! How?"

The Man With No Eyes shrugged.

Neg considered the information. That the man knew was no mystery. They had some kind of link among them. But—what was he to do? Obviously, they had found Tuanne, and had been slain for their trouble. They must be close to her still. He could send more priests, or . . .

Neg spun away and stalked toward his Spell Chamber. Unless the bodies of the killed priests had been burned or hacked to bits, they could still be useful. He would recall their souls from the Gray Lands and reanimate their bodies. Whoever had dealt them the death-cards would find dealing with zombies much more difficult. . . .

Conan, Elashi, and Tuanne, now mounted on solid horses and bearing food, blankets, and assorted utensils strapped to their mounts, approached the South Gate of Opkothard. The guard there was the same who had been working earlier, when Skeer made his escape. The man recognized Conan, and said not a word, merely ordered that the gate be opened.

With the night half done, the Cimmerian youth, the desert woman, and the beautiful zombie departed the city of spiders.

The Opkothardian morgue had been dug deep into the earth, so that the heat of the sun would not accelerate the decay of its occupants. It was both cool and dark, even at noon, and as the hour approached midnight, the only light came from flickering fat lamps set in sconces here and there on the walls. The air was mostly still, but shadows danced on the dark walls as the fat sputtered and sent smoky tendrils toward the low ceiling.

The attendant sat propped on a high-backed stool, leaning back against the wall nearest the door, contemplating his next meal. He had cheese and wine and even some fresh fruit, and he debated with himself as to which he should devour first, and when. He had been busy earlier. There were eight new bodies, all dead of violence, to be palleted and tagged for burial. Six of them blind men, now there was an unusual happenstance. In his twelve years running the morgue, he had seen corpses aplenty, but never six so alike, and blind to boot. Then there was the priest from up the mountains, the Ulblats or Oblates or some such. Finally, there was the nightwatchman, with his caved-in skull and slit throat. Somebody out there with a lust for blood, right enough.

The cheese, he decided, washed down with the wine. He would save the fruit for later.

As he unwrapped the cheese, something disturbed the flies.

Normally, there were not many flies in the morgue. The attendant did not much care for them buzzing over his charges. A few managed to slip in now and then, and eventually, when he was bored enough, he would hunt them down and swat them. Mostly, they were no bother. Now and again, a gas bubble would shake a corpse, and rattle the flies enough so they would buzz around a moment before alighting again. Likely that was the cause of the buzzing he now heard.

Odd, though, he thought, as he sliced a chunk of the cheese with his knife and popped it into his mouth. A trick of the flickering light made it look like one of the cadavers in the back corner had moved.

He chuckled. That had happened a time or two. Somebody they thought dead came out of a deep trancelike sleep. None of these bodies were going to do that, though. None of them had any illness claim them; 'twas cold steel and hard brick that done 'em in, and none were ever deader.

The flies buzzed again. Very loudly this time.

The attendant sat up, clutching his cheese knife. Could maybe a rat have gotten in? Set-damned rats! He hated them. He slid from the stool. Best go see.

He was bent over, searching the floor for any sign of rodents when one of the blind men sat up.

The attendant jumped high enough to smack his head on the ceiling. Gas, it had to be—

One by one, the other blind dead men began to stir.

When one of them slipped from the pallet and stood, turning his head from side to side, the attendant ran, dropping his cheese and knife, screaming. This was black evil and nothing else!

When the attendant had done, the Men With No Eyes filed silently out of the morgue, saying nothing, united once again in their purpose. They sought one like them, and this time, they would have her or live forever as zombies.

Skeer rode at a gallop until the horse, exhausted, could do no more than walk. The vision of the spiders had caused in him more panic than he could remember ever feeling, but now that he was far away from the city, he felt better. A little better, but—if knowledge was power, then Skeer's weakness rivaled that of a newborn babe. Whatever had happened back in Opkothard lay beyond his ability to understand at the moment. His temptation was to rein in his stolen mount, find some small creature for bloodletting, and try to contact Neg. Years of self-preservation and caution held that thought in check, however. There seemed to be some treachery afoot, and Neg might well be involved in it. Skeer had not managed to survive this long by trusting anyone.

Once he arrived at his destination, Neg's stronghold near the fabled Triple Juncture of Corinthia, Zamora, and Koth, he could survey the lay of his situation. He had friends—well, at least those who would supply information for a heavy stipend—who could apprise him of Neg's demeanor. From that position he could proceed accordingly.

Likely, some mistake lay at the root of all that insanity back in the walled city. It would be properly rectified when he arrived at Neg's castle. But just in case things were not as he wished, he would move as the sharp-spined anteater did when making love in the old joke: slowly and with great care.

A chill wind touched him, and he pulled the stolen cape closer about his shoulders.

"We ride for a hour or two, then make camp," Conan said.

Elashi said, "I thought we could travel at night, that the road was clear and wide."

"Skeer must sleep eventually. So must we. You and I, at least."

But it was only three-quarters of that time later that Conan pulled his mount to a halt. He stared off into the darkness, then turned to Elashi.

"Those spiders prefer warmth, you said?"

"They are common in the desert, yes. Such cold air as this would certainly disable or destroy them."

"I think not. Look."

Elashi seemed to strain her eyes against the darkness. "I see nothing, save a small mound."

Conan turned to Tuanne.

"I see them," she said quietly.

"Them? Where?" Elashi raised herself higher upon her saddle, using her knees against the horse's back. Conan noted the play of strong muscle in her legs as her split skirt shifted to reveal her thighs.

"The mound," the Cimmerian said. "Watch it carefully."

A moment passed. Then, "It moves!"

"Aye. It is composed of the spiders. Perhaps those on the outside might expire in the night air, but I think maybe those within might well survive."

"Spiders do not behave so!"

"Normal spiders do not," Tuanne said. "These are enspelled. They have a purpose."

Elashi shuddered, and Conan felt a chill crawl along his own spine. He would not like to be the object of those enchanted creatures.

"We shall move back down the road for our camp."

"A good ways, I hope?" Elashi said.

"Aye."

Thirteen

The clothing used to tie him had been childishly easy to escape from, but not so the emotions that dogged him. Even the night could not hide the Disguise Master's humiliation; he felt as if it glowed from him, beckoning to any passerby: see, I am shamed by a barbarian! The agony of it chewed at him, like some unseen rodent, sharp teeth drawing constant professional blood. In twenty winters, he had never been seen for what he was while he plied his trade. True, those with natural suspicion had looked upon him askance, but then, they looked upon everyone that way. No one had ever entrapped him as had the muscle-bound outlander, no one had ever seen him for what he was. It had always been a point of high pride with him. But now, he could no longer carry that unblemished affirmation. And worse, after the ultimate insult, that barbaric lout had robbed him!

The Disguise Master stalked the night streets, enraged. The money was nothing. He had amassed a fortune over the years, had more than he could ever spend. Gold meant nothing. Craft was the thing, craft and honor. And now,

132

his honor stood in ruins. A single spot of black amidst all the white had turned it gray. True, one man out of thousands could hardly be considered monumental failure, but gray was still gray, no matter how light the hue.

What was he to do?

The solution seemed obvious. As long as the barbarian— Conan, he called himself—walked the land of the living, the Disguise Master's honor could not be cleansed. Alive, he was a blot. Dead, the statement could be made: No living man can claim to have bested the Disguise Master.

Yes. That offered the only respite.

He himself had killed now and again, but he was no assassin. But he had more money than he could possibly spend, and there were those more adept at striking a man down than he, those who would do so gladly for sufficient payment.

The priest was shut of the whole matter now that the participants had departed his city. But honor must be served. He would rectify the matter, even if he had to travel to the end of the Earth to do it. He would watch the barbarian squirm before he had him killed. The Disguise Master smiled. There lay a pleasant thought. Conan of Barbaria dead, and the Disguise Master's honor reclaimed.

He would gather men and supplies and leave as soon as possible.

Elashi screamed.

Conan came up from sleep, sword in hand, looking for the threat. It proved to be easy enough to dispatch when he found it.

One of the black spiders scuttled from Elashi's blanket. Before it moved far, Conan trod upon it. It made a crackling, pulpy sound as he crushed it.

When Conan turned back toward Elashi, he found his two female companions hugging each other tightly.

"It was only a single spider," he said. "Likely lost from the main group."

"I hate them!" Elashi said. Then, after a moment, she said, "Tuanne, you are so *cold*!"

The pale-skinned woman nodded. "I have been cold for as long as I remember, it seems. It is an ache one learns to stand; it never becomes comfortable."

For a moment, no one spoke. Then, Elashi looked up at Conan. She raised one knee slightly, and her skirt fell back to reveal her shapely thigh, tanned brown by the sun. Her skin contrasted darkly next to Tuanne's, and the effect struck Conan in such a way that he found his breath coming faster.

"She is cold, Conan. Come, and help me warm her."

At first, the young Cimmerian took her meaning simply. But when Elashi moved her knees farther apart, raising her skirt so that he could see clearly her dark triangle, it dawned on him that her intent went past merely warming Tuanne. It was an invitation he did not expect, sudden in its tendering, but also one he did not intend to refuse. He did not question her change of heart—he had yet to meet the man who understood why women behaved as they did.

"Aye," he said, sheathing his iron sword, "we shall all warm each other."

Both Tuanne and Elashi smiled, and Conan also grinned as he went to join them under the blankets.

The Brute stank of wine and sweat, but the Disguise Master minded it little; after all, the man was a killer, and supposedly the best in the city. He had plied his trade for some six years, and that he still lived surely meant he was adept at it. According to his sources, the Brute—if he had another name, no one seemed aware of it—had slain in personal combat some seventeen men; additionally, he had backstabbed twice that many more. He was big, dirty, brutal, and coarse. Exactly what the Disguise Master desired for this particular job.

As the dawn's light painted the skies, the Disguise Master readied his crew. Along with the Brute, he had engaged a pair of footpads whose skills ran more to petty thievery than to mayhem, but who would do anything for money. Murder seemed no barrier, and he would have trusted them less than the distance he could heave them, without the Brute as protection. The latter might slay him for his gold easily, save that he had been promised a large sum on the return to Opkothard, and the Disguise Master had made certain that his party knew he carried only small coinage upon his person. Alive and back in the city, he would be worth money; dead on the trail would serve no one.

It had taken no small effort to learn all there was to know about Skeer, and the knowledge gained left much to be desired. Still, where he was bound seemed known: he was likely a minion of the necromancer Neg, about whom little good could be said. This was inference, but the presence of the woman zombie and the raising of the six dead men from the morgue gave truth to some form of necromancy. And, since Neg the Malefic was the leading exponent of this form of magic anywhere close to the city, then likely Neg's hand lay upon the proceedings in some manner. His castle was known, even in Opkothard, and if Skeer traveled there, his pursurer Conan must surely follow. Therefore, to find his quarry, the Disguise Master need only travel to Neg's domain. Somewhere along the way, perhaps, they would happen across the doomed Cimmerian. If not, they could await his arrival. A simple plan, and like most of his plans, most workable.

Feeling his confidence return, the Disguise Master led his motley entourage through the South Gate of Opkothard and into the morning light.

The new sun aborning caught Skeer in the grip of a nightmare: he was buried under thousands of crawly spiders, being bitten and injected with venom that burned in his veins like acid. . . .

Skeer sat up suddenly, cold sweat beaded on his face. Spiders—!

He shuddered in the chill air. A dream. It was only a dream.

Nonetheless, Skeer hurried to gather up his blankets and to stoke up a quick fire for breakfast. There seemed no way that spiders, no matter how determined, could follow him through the cold mountain passes. In less than a week, he would be in Neg's domain, and that worthy magician's magic surely was proof against any threat that might be dogging him, arachnidal or human.

They marched together, footfalls landing in uniform cadence, six who had been alive but now were animated by necromantic mantology. Dead the Men With No Eyes were, but moving inexorably after their assigned quarry. They did not rest, neither did they stop for food or drink.

The dead have no need for such things.

In his cleanest of rooms Neg paused in his movements to stroke the spire of crystal that occupied the center of the marble-walled temple. Soon, he would have the power to bring this room to its function. Soon, he would be not merely Neg the Malefic, but Neg the Omnipotent.

He smiled, feeling the cold crystal under his fingers. Yes, the promise of it touched him almost orgasmically, a thing he had not known in itself for hundreds of that years. Power. Power was the best aphrodisiac. When he had that power, he would call Tuanne to him and make use of her as he had never been able to before. Yes.

Conan awoke with an arm around each of the women. Elashi, in his left, was warm, her breath tickling his bare chest lightly. Tuanne, much less cold than before, lay quietly curled against his right side, her lips pressed against his skin gently.

The young Cimmerian had never spent such a night before, and the memory of it brought a smile and a catlike satisfaction to his thoughts. He would revise his opinion of traveling with two women, to be certain.

Elashi woke, and Tuanne's eyes opened. They lifted their heads and smiled across Conan's broad chest at each other, then at him.

"Sleep well, Conan?" Elashi asked.

"Never better."

Tuanne said, "I have not been warmer in a hundred years. Thank you, both."

"Anytime," Conan said. "If you are feeling a chill at the moment . . . ?"

Elashi swatted his shoulder. "Goat!"

Conan grinned. Not a goat, perhaps, but not found wanting, at least. Pride stirred within him.

Within a few moments, Conan started a fire, upon which a quick meal was prepared. Again there was no meat, it being difficult to carry other than dried without spoiling, but there was bread and cheese and hot herbed water to drive away the earliness of the hour.

After clearing the camp and loading the horses, the three departed.

Farther up the road, they paused at the spot where they had seen the spiders the previous night.

Only a few arachnid carcasses remained, quivering in the sun's early rays, or being picked apart by carrion feeders, ravens, and larger vultures.

"They have departed ahead of us," Conan said. "Save the ones who were exposed to the cold directly."

Elashi said, "Ooh. It makes me shiver to think of all those black creatures scuttling along!"

"Think how you would feel if you knew they pursued you instead of Skeer," Tuanne said.

"An unpleasant thought," Conan said.

Indeed. He would not wish such a fate upon any man, even Skeer. His plans for the brigand included merely an appointment with a sword, a clean and honorable end. Perhaps better than Skeer merited, given the list of offenses of which Conan personally knew; still, magic was better left alone, and Conan would not curse Skeer with such a fate as some spider-god had done.

Fourteen

The days passed quickly for Skeer. He slept little, stopping only when the obnubilation of darkness forced him to rein his tired horse to a halt. He would rise with first light, eat of his sparse supplies, and resume his journey. He looked back frequently, but saw nothing threatening. The weight of the magical talisman in his purse seemed to increase each day, but his hard riding brought him closer to Neg's domain with each of his mount's footfalls. Another day, and he would be in territory where he was known and respected as one of Neg's own. Another day.

"We near the village that is the gateway to Neg's domain," Tuanne said. "I can feel his presence ahead of us like some malignant beacon."

"Skeer pushes himself. We have gained but little," Conan said.

Elashi said, "I would catch him, but I must confess that I look forward to nights now."

Conan grinned. He, too, did not mind the coming of

darkness, not with Tuanne and Elashi to bracket him as
they lay together.

Neg could feel the approach of the Source of Light, as a
cold man might feel the warmth of a distant fire. It was
only a glimmer now, the faintest of heats, but it came.

He stood in the ingress of one of the high tower win-
dows, watching a thunderstorm spend its fury upon the
castle and surrounding land. Lightning turned the night
into stark day for a heartbeat, and thunder punctuated the
flash with the voice of an angry giant. Torrents of rain
swept over the ancient stone of his castle, wafting that
unique dusty smell to his nostrils on the wings of the damp
wind.

Soon the land would ring of steel and boots, as he
commanded a different kind of thunder, that of the marching dead. Soon.

Dead, the six Men With No Eyes marched stolidly, stoic
in the face of the angry storm. They moved as always,
slowed only by the mud and wind. They had no supernatural speed, but like a tortoise, they continued relentlessly.
What they lost to the horses, they regained during the
night, so that they drew closer, albeit slowly, to her whom
they sought. Where she journeyed was of no import, neither
did it matter how long it took to make up the distance.

Eventually, they would prevail, even had they to walk
to the ends of the Earth. Or beyond.

Brute grumbled. "Gods-be-damned rain!"

The tarp over his conical head leaked, spilling a trickle
of cold water onto his neck, and he shifted his position,

shoving one of the sniveling footpads halfway out into the deluge.

"Hey, hey!" the man said.

The Disguise Master did not know the man's real name, if he had one, but called him "Port," since it seemed he always took the left when they traveled. The other one naturally became "Starboard." For a well-remembered and detested year, the Disguise Master had been impressed into a ship's gang, sailing the dog routes across the Vilayet Sea to the Eastern Cities of Turan: Khoraf, Khorusun, Onagrul, and half a dozen smaller ports. He knew sailing terms well, and sometimes used them as part of his costume when disguised as a seaman.

Brute turned to glare at the protesting man. "Something you wished to say, rat-eater?"

Port took little time to consider his reply. "Nay, Captain. I 'uz just startled, 's all."

Brute turned away, uninterested. The Disguise Master had restrained the man from killing both Port and Starboard several times. Good. The more irritated he got, the worse for Conan when they caught him. Which, he hoped, would be soon. He cared little for the rain, and his tarp fared only slightly better than the one under which Brute hunkered.

Once, during a lull in the mostly-steady rain, Conan arose from the communal arrangement with Tuanne and Elashi to attend to a function of nature. As he avoided the larger puddles outside their strung-and-staked tent, he saw something scuttle across the wet ground. A rat? Or a ground squirrel—?

No.

He was slow to move, and the creature escaped his boot

and vanished into the wet night. He finished his business and returned to the makeshift tent. Elashi stirred and smiled at him. Sleepily, she said, "Everything all right?"

"Aye," he replied.

He did not mention the eight-legged denizen he had seen. There seemed no point in so doing.

But a glance at Tuanne's dark eyes showed that she had seen what he had.

It had many names, the village. It was sometimes called "Vanatta," in honor of a local man who had proved himself adept in politics a hundred years past, becoming advisor to the then-king. Those distant workers of magic familiar with Neg's proximity tended to call it "Necromancer's Hold." The villagers, when they bothered, usually just called the place "Rain Town," for the long season of storms that seemed to always find the village even when the surrounding countryside stayed dry. Many blamed the constant rain on Neg's influence, but few dared to speak such a thing aloud. Even the dead had ears, and no man wished to call necromantic attention to himself by speaking ill of the local wizard.

Skeer cared nothing for the names, and thought little of the village at all, but never had he been so glad to see it as he was on this evening. He had friends here, or at least comrades willing to help him, either for Neg's favor or hard cash.

It was to the smallest of the town's three inns that he rode, saddle-weary and edgy from lack of sleep. Darkness had begun to claim the day, but at last the damned rain had ceased. At the inn, Skeer flung the horse's reins at the stoop boy. "Care for the animal," he said.

"Aye, my lord Skeer! And fine to see you, sir!"

Skeer ignored the boy and tromped through the mud to the inn's entrance. It was called "The Boiled Pig," for reasons known only to the first owner, long dead, and as such places went, it would take either major reconstruction or burning down to improve it. "Pig's Sty" would be a better name, but even so, he welcomed it. The Boiled Pig offered safety. Anyone who asked for him here would meet bland looks and raised brows. Skeer? No one here by that name. No one arrived here of late at all. Perhaps you might try the Necropolis, or the Smoking Cat. . . .

Inside, the innkeep, a large man bearing several scars on his face from his years as a soldier, nodded at Skeer.

"A room," Skeer said. "And a bottle, with a woman to bring it and stay. You have not seen me."

Scarface nodded. "Take four," he said. "Imelda will deliver your wine."

Skeer nodded. Imelda kept herself relatively clean, talked little, and asked no questions. Good. What he wanted now was company and sleep, more the latter than the former, a measure of how tired he was.

Skeer shuffled over the sawdust floor toward the room. There was no talk of money, nor would there be any: Skeer held a half interest in The Boiled Pig, and such a thing entitled him to some privileges.

In the morning he would ask questions, to discern, if possible, Neg's current mood. But first he would rest.

As night stole the light from the skies, Conan, Elashi, and Tuanne came to an unexpected halt. Ahead lay a deep ravine, at the bottom of which ran the fast-moving waters of a river. There had been a bridge constructed of thick ropes and planks over the ravine, but the anchoring posts on Conan's side of the drop had weakened, from the storm, apparently, and one of the logs had pulled loose from the wet earth. A single strand of arm-thick hemp stretched across the abyss to the remaining post, itself leaning precariously; the other post lay on a ledge a hundred feet down, and the ropes to which it had been attached dangled near it.

"Oh," Elashi said. "We shall have to go around."

Tuanne shook her head. "It is fifty miles to the next bridge—if it still hangs."

Conan dismounted and peered over the edge of the cliff. He stood, brushed mud from his hands, and began to look around.

"For what are you searching?" Tuanne said.

"There would be spare rope for repairs, if the bridge builders had any foresight. Protected from rot, I'll wager."

"What good would that do?" Elashi asked. "There are no trees thick enough to support the weight of the bridge anywhere around here. And the ropes are out of reach."

"Ah," the young Cimmerian said, "there is a box sheltered in those rocks. Let us see what it contains."

As Conan had guessed, the thick wooden box, sealed with some rancid oil, proved to contain several lengths of hemp of various diameters. Conan began to coil one of the lines, somewhat thicker than his thumb, into a series of hoops.

"In Cimmeria, we learn to climb before we can walk. I shall climb down and attach the rope to the post. Our horses can pull the post up, we shall replant it, restring the bridge, and go on our way."

"What about the ropes on the bridge?" Elashi said.

"A simple matter. I shall climb out and fetch them back."

"In the dark?"

He laughed. "Morning would be better. Even a Cimmerian avoids climbing on wet rock in the dark unless there is a compelling hurry to do so."

"Perhaps we should bed early," Elashi said, "so that you will be strong in the morning?"

Conan smiled at her, then at Tuanne. "Aye. A good idea."

In the morning, Conan arose, feeling much refreshed and very strong. While the two women fixed breakfast, he tied one end of the coil of thick rope to the remaining bridge support, after hammering the pole upright with a head-sized boulder, then tossed the rope over the cliff and began his descent into the gorge.

The rocks were somewhat drier after the night without rain, and the footholds were many, so it took only a few minutes to make the climb down to the fallen post. Once the rope was attached to the fallen support, it was but a matter of a few more moments for him to scramble up the hemp hand over hand.

It took longer to weave a makeshift harness for the three horses, but before the sun had risen far on his day's journey across the heavens, the fallen bridge support was raised. Conan's muscles bulged as he helped the horses drag the post to its former place of residence, upending the thick wood into the soggy hole.

Another two hours work saw the two posts firmly implanted in the ground, with heavy rocks to aid the tamping and support.

Finally, Conan climbed out onto the bridge on the single line, swinging like a monkey until he reached the wooden planking, then dangling down to snatch at the free-swinging lines.

By noon, the structure's repair was accomplished. Conan's skill with rope came from years of practical application, and the knots were pulled tight not only by his own mighty thews, but by those of the horses, as well. Likely the bridge was as strong as it had ever been, he figured.

But as they began to cross the bridge, Tuanne turned sharply in her saddle to look behind them.

Conan said, "What—?"

"The Men With No Eyes!"

He turned to see six forms approaching at a run, all moving in eerie unison. He reached for his sword.

"Conan, no! They are dead—like me. Your blade will be useless!"

"I'll take off their heads! Let them find us without them!"

Elashi said, "There is a better way!"

Conan turned to stare at her. She held one hand stiff, pointing down at the bridge upon which their horses now stood. Conan understood instantly. "Good idea."

The Cimmerian giant dug his heels into his horse's sides, and the animal started forward.

Once on the opposite side of the bridge, Conan quickly dismounted as the women thundered past. He drew his blade, and waited. Timing would be important. A shame to waste all the morning's work, though.

The six zombies broke into two files of three each as they approached the bridge, saying nothing Conan could hear. Their feet hit the first planks. He waited.

The first two were halfway across before the last two started onto the bridge. Conan waited.

The leaders were no more than three spans away. Conan raised his sword, still waiting. Two spans, one—now!

Using the strength of his arm and chest, Conan swung the sword. The razored blue iron bit into the support rope and sheared it cleanly. The bridge tilted abruptly, canting sharply as the support on one side let go.

Three of the Men With No Eyes pitched off into the abyss, falling silently. The other three were quicker, and they grabbed onto the planks, saving themselves from the fall.

In another stroke, Conan sheared the center support rope. Hemp unraveled as the rope snapped, tilting the bridge yet farther from level. Another of the zombie priests lost his grip and slid off to join his brothers.

The remaining two began to inch their way along the precarious platform toward Conan.

The Cimmerian's sword rose for the third time. The final cut took the final rope, and the bridge, anchored only at the far side, swung down and across the chasm, to smash into the cliff Conan had climbed down and up earlier in the day. The heavy wooden planks split and shattered from the force of the pendulum swing, and the final two passengers were knocked from their perch, to tumble to the river far below.

Behind him, Tuanne said, "The fall will not destroy them."

Conan turned and nodded at her. "Perhaps not. But it will surely slow them. Even a Cimmerian could not make that climb in less than a day or two. By then we shall be well on our way."

He mounted his horse; after a moment the three of them rode away.

Skeer awoke, feeling more refreshed than he had in months, it seemed. Nothing like a safe roof over one's head, a warm body in one's bed, and wine in one's belly to allay nagging unease.

A breakfast warming his insides, Skeer began to ascertain the state of affairs in the village, and, more important, with his master, Neg the Malefic.

From One-Eye the cutpurse, he heard: "Nay, 'tain't nothin' unusual about His Lordship's domain. They that don't see come and go like usual."

From Alleta the trull, came: "I cannot speak for his desire, since it seems he has no taste for the pleasures of the flesh, but, no, nothing to indicate any strangeness other than normal have I seen."

More informative was Piper, the store's lackey: "Sure, sure, I been inside, just like always. What? No, his worship don't seem angry, 'cept that one of his Reawakened Ones got loose, somehows. No, he didn' make that privy to me, but a man's got ears, ain't he? Other than that, no different than usual, I say."

Skeer considered the sources, naturally, when digesting the information that he had been fed. And he did not stop with just those three, but after the greater part of the morning nosing around and asking such questions of a dozen others, including some of the less criminally minded citizens of the village, he felt that the comments he had first heard were representative. Few people actually saw Neg, only a few suppliers of goods and services, but all of them seemed to think the necromancer's state of mind differed little than usual. While Neg could hardly be termed "usual" or "normal" when compared to other men, he had emotions, and they did not seem particularly stirred.

Good. With that assurance, Skeer felt he had dallied enough. Another day in the village without attending to his given chore would be dangerous, for certainly Neg would learn of it. And he had said most plainly to make all deliberate speed. A night of rest from an exhausting and dangerous trip could be justified. A day of dithering afterward could not.

With his courage bolstered, Skeer squared his narrow shoulders and went to meet his master.

Fifteen

The village lay before Conan and his companions, and it seemed little different from a dozen other such hamlets the Cimmerian had seen before. But he reined his mount to a halt when he saw what lay beyond the sleepy-looking town. Few cities of any size were likely to sport such a castle as he now saw.

Vast it was, and ancient; time had weathered the dark gray stone so that it seemed almost smooth from this distance, but even the years could not wash the evil that emanated from that massive edifice. Conan felt his skin crawl as the hairs stood on his arms and neck. He had an urgent desire to turn and ride as fast as the horse could run, a gut feeling that stole over him as he stared at the tall towers and high walls.

"Neg's castle," Tuanne said unnecessarily.

Elashi said, "I suppose it is too much to ask of the gods that Skeer has yet to gain entrance to that—that fortress."

Tuanne nodded. "It is. I can feel the pull of the talisman, and it lies beyond those walls."

Conan uttered a short curse that he deemed inappropri-

ate for the ears of his companions, so he spoke the expletive under his breath. Well. There was nothing to be done
for it. If that was where Skeer had gone, then that was
where *he* would go, too.

"Do you know a way in?" he asked Tuanne.

"I knew a way out. But I suspect that path will be
blocked. Doubtless Neg has discovered it, once he learned
that I had escaped his clutches."

Conan turned back to stare at the castle. He could not
see the base at this distance, but there would be a way
inside, and if he looked diligently enough, he would find
it.

Tuanne seemed to read his thoughts. "I am afraid gaining entrance will be no small matter," she said. "Neg is
jealous of his privacy. And I cannot offer much assistance
in this. I am free of his spell only by a magical fluke.
Should he see me, he could resume his ensorcellment of
me easier than scratching a bothersome itch."

"Let us find an inn, then. We have money and can book
a room and eat before we decide our best path." Conan
turned away from the distant castle.

Silently, the two women followed the Cimmerian into
the village.

Despite his assurances, Skeer felt a prickle of fear as he
approached the only entrance to Neg's castle. *Some*thing
was in the air. He felt it, with the sense that every good
thief had, a high tension, as if some giant string had been
stretched to near its breaking point. Outwardly, things seemed
the same as when he had last been there; but there lay
beneath the normal sights another thing altogether.

The moat seemed sluggish in the afternoon sun, but
beneath those placid waters swam creatures better left

unprovoked. Fish as big as a man with teeth the size of a man's fingers lurked, awaiting feeding, intentional or otherwise. And in the depths, so he had heard, monsters that fed on the killer fish made *them* seem like minnows.

Once, so the story went, a curious and mostly insane soldier had determined to row a boat across the ring of infested water, with the idea of scaling the castle wall and slaying Neg, for some injury Neg had caused to himself or his family. Armed with sword and pike, the soldier had a sturdy wooden pirogue unloaded from his wagon and into the water.

Halfway across the moat, the soldier met his fate. He sank in a bloody swirl of water and vanished forever, boat and all.

Since, no one had been eager to attempt a crossing of the wizard's deadly ditch, as it was known locally.

The tall drawbridge nestled against the stone when Skeer approached. When he was close to the edge of the moat, the massive bridge began to descend, the heavy chains rattling as they passed through the iron-ringed portals, despite the thick layers of grease there. He had not called out his name, but it was not necessary. Though blind, the Men With No Eyes knew Skeer; whether by smell or hearing or some other arcane manner, it did not matter.

The drawbridge finished its descent. Skeer looked up, and a score of Neg's priests peered sightlessly down over the wall's top at him. He repressed a shudder. He had learned to tolerate Neg's other servants, but the Men With No Eyes frightened him more than even the zombie dead.

He hesitated for a moment, then nudged his horse forward. It was much too late to turn back. Besides, he told himself, he had something that Neg wanted more than anything. He had served the necromancer exceedingly well, and would no doubt be most welcome.

Brute exited the inn and looked up at the Disguise Master. "Ain't here," the big and smelly man said.

The Disguise Master nodded. "That leaves only one inn, the Smoking Cat. If they have arrived before us, likely we shall find them there."

"Good," Brute said.

But at the final inn boasted by the village, Conan of Cimmeria was not to be found. There were, however, the two women who had aided in humiliating the Disguise Master.

Outside, the professional spy said, "Take the women. Surely Conan intends to return for them."

Brute shook his head. "I'll not have anything to do with that pale one."

"What?"

"She carries some kind of curse, and I'll not infect myself with it."

"I am paying you—"

"—to kill the big man, no more."

"We'll do it," Port said.

The Disguise Master looked at the footpad. "You?"

"Him and me," Port said, nodding at Starboard. The second man nodded his affirmation.

The Disguise Master looked at Brute in disgust. The big man shrugged blandly. "No matter to me. I'll do Conan."

"Very well. Bring the women to me. I shall wait behind the stables, there."

"Aye, master," Port and Starboard said in unison.

Inside the Inn, Elashi and Tuanne rested in the room

they had taken. Conan had gone to inspect the defenses of Neg's castle. He would, he had said, return before dawn.

"I must go to the nightchamber," Elashi said.

Tuanne said, "I shall wait here."

"I think I envy you that, not having to attend to such needs."

"Do not," Tuanne said. "It hardly makes up for the rest."

"I suppose not. I shall return shortly."

Though she carried her dagger, the attack by two small men caught Elashi unawares. Before she could defend herself, one of the attackers had his own dagger's point pressed into her throat. "Move wrongly and die!" he said.

"What is it you wish? I have no money—"

"Not money, bitch. Neither do we desire your favors. Our master would have a word with you."

The other one said, "Can you handle her?"

"Certainly I can, fool. Fetch the other one."

The door to the room opened, and where Tuanne expected to see Elashi, she saw a strange man. At first, she thought perhaps he was one of Neg's, but his manner lacked the confidence one of the necromancer's minions would have this close to home. He held a short dagger pointed in her general direction.

Conan had provided Tuanne with a dagger of her own upon leaving Opkothard. She snatched the blade from her belt and faced the intruder. He smiled, a wicked, gap-toothed grin, and moved slowly toward her.

Tuanne's own smile rose, and wicked was too mild a term for it. This one carried his confidence in his blade. That could be destroyed.

Slowly, Tuanne raised her left arm, so that the sleeve of

her blouse slid back, revealing the cold ivory flesh. Just as slowly, she lifted the dagger so that the keen edge lay against the flesh of the raised arm.

The intruder paused. She could almost hear his thoughts: Hey, what is this?

With a quick motion that made him jump, she sliced her arm. The wound gaped, but no blood flowed. She felt the sting of the cold steel, then felt the edges of the cut begin to seal shut and heal. The process took only a few seconds.

"Great Asura!" The man backed away, holding both hands out in front of himself, the knife he held obviously forgotten in his fear.

Tuanne tossed her own knife underhanded toward the room's nearest wall. As luck had it, the instrument struck point first and quivered in the wood. She began to advance toward the frightened man. "Come," she said. "Let me touch you and drink your life."

At that, the man turned and nearly slammed into the wall in his haste to escape. Before she took a second step, he was gone, more fleet than a rabbit from a hound.

She smiled, amused by the incident, until she remembered that Elashi had not returned. The amusement vanished as Tuanne darted into the hall, seeking her companion. A quick circuit of the inn revealed that which she feared: Elashi was gone.

Crouched in a stand of tall reeds on the edge of the necromancer's moat, Conan studied the walls of the castle. The blocks had been quarried and set without mortar, and the centuries of rain had blended the joinings into a smooth facing. An ordinary man would have little success climbing such a wall, but Conan felt certain of his ability to do so, although it would be a difficult ascent, even for him.

Guards patrolled the top, more of the blind ones, and their number was not small. Since they did not see as such, they might well hear the scrabblings of his fingertips as he scaled the wall, and that would be bad. Clinging like a fly to a flat wall was not the best position from which to defend one's self. Even an indifferent marksman could pick him off with a crossbow from the top, should they ''see'' him attempting the climb. Or a pot of hot oil could do wonders for defense, were it poured upon a hapless climber.

When the guards had passed, the young Cimmerian found a hand-sized rock among the reeds. He hefted it, then lobbed it overhead, so that it struck the moat near the center.

The resulting agitation of the water, terminating in the leap of some monster fish nearly as big as he was, told Conan what he wished to know: swimming or rowing across *that* body of water would be a fool's venture.

He slipped away from the reeds, moving quietly for all his size, until he had gained the cover of a small copse nearby. Gaining entry to the castle would be no easy matter, as Tuanne had said. Already, he had determined that the tunnel she had used to escape from the necromancer's chambers had been sealed with earth, to a depth as far as Conan's sword would reach, at least. The moat boasted those monsters, and the walls were only slightly less smooth than a baby's backside. Darkness would offer no cover, not to guards without eyes. It posed a tricky problem, fair enough.

Conan worked his way through the thin growth to where he had tied his horse. No, it would be no easy task. Of course, he could set up camp and wait for Skeer to leave, but if Tuanne was correct, they had not the time. With the magical device Skeer would have tendered to his master, the dead would be stirring, and that thought gave the Cimmerian youth no comfort. Besides, he did not have the patience to stand idly by and wait. A man of action could grow old waiting. No, there would have to be some way. He could not see it at this point, but if one existed, he would find it.

For now, he would return to the inn.

"Where is Elashi?"

"Taken," Tuanne said.

"Taken? Where? By whom?"

Quickly, she explained. Before she had finished, Conan was on his way outside. She followed.

The late afternoon sun had vanished behind a thick bank of slate clouds, building to a storm in the west. A wind had begun, and the air seemed alive with energy when the Cimmerian stepped into the street. Just ahead of him, Conan saw a big man, larger even than himself, holding a thick broadsword, point down. That he awaited Conan seemed all too obvious. At the sight of Conan, the man raised his blade.

Conan drew his own sword without question. A man pointing a blade at you needed no explanation until afterward, assuming you survived to ask about his reasons.

But the big man offered an expository greeting.

"Conan of Cimmeria, be you?"

"Aye. Have I business with you?"

"Indeed. My master, him who you made sport of in Opkothard, bids me to tell you that he hopes you enjoyed your stolen gold, for it shall cost you your life."

"The spy."

"He prefers the name Disguise Master."

"Has he taken my companion, Elashi, of the desert?"

"Aye, that he has."

"Then he is dog and son of a dog!" Conan said.

The big man grinned at the Cimmerian. "You'll not anger me so easy, boy. He is not family, only paymaster."

Conan stalked forward, his sword held with the point aimed at the other man's throat.

"Tell me where Elashi is and live," Conan said.

The big man facing the Cimmerian laughed. "For all your size, you are no more than a boy to me, barbarian. You shall be dead in a moment, what matters where your woman might be?"

Conan inched closer, his boots set solidly upon the packed earth of the road, his knees bent slightly, ready to spring. He was finished talking.

The big man lunged at Conan, swiping at him with the broadsword in a wide slash that would have taken his head from his body, had it landed. Rather than trying to block, the Cimmerian ducked under the cut and thrust with his own sword.

The big man danced back quickly, and Conan's stab fell a foot short of its target. The Cimmerian youth did not pause, but followed the thrust with a full overhead swing, as a man swings an axe for splitting wood.

The big man raised his blade to block, and the *clang!* of metal on metal produced sparks visible even in the brightness of the day. Conan felt the vibration of the blades begin in his wrists and run all the way to his shoulders. The man was strong, no denying that.

His opponent shifted to his right, and duplicated Conan's overhead cut. Instead of blocking, Conan danced to his right and parried, slamming his blade into the flat of the big man's sword. The attacker's sword missed Conan cleanly, and such was the force of the strike that it carried the broadsword in an arc that buried the tip in the dirt of the street.

Before Conan could follow up, however, the man wrenched his weapon free and turned to face the Cimmerian once again.

"Not bad for a boy, and a barbarian, to boot," the big man said. "I would have you know the name of your slayer, Conan. I am called Brute."

Conan spared Brute a choppy nod, but no words. The man stood between him and Elashi, and whatever respect he might feel for Brute as a fighter was tempered by his disdain for him as a kidnapper.

Brute charged, swinging his blade back and forth like a fan.

Conan backed away, his own sword raised high. One step, two, three. He caught the rhythm of Brute's powerful swings one-two, one-two, and mentally set himself.

On Brute's backswing Conan moved. Instead of backing, he leaped in, slightly aslant to Brute's recovery slash. With all the power he could muster, Conan brought his weapon down—

The razored iron clawed Brute's arm just below the thick muscle of his shoulder, sliced through the flesh and bone, and cut into the ribs beneath, stopping before they were sheared through.

"Ahhh!"

Brute's arm gouted blood and was flung away from his body by the weight of the broadsword still clutched in his hand. For a heartbeat, Brute held the hilt of his weapon in his remaining hand, with the severed arm and hand also attached to the sword's grip. Then, the sword and arm fell away, as the shock hit him. Brute fell to his knees, his life pumping into the street. He made a vain attempt to stop the flow with his hand, but it was futile; blood ran past the hand, which rapidly grew ghostly.

Brute looked at Conan, and managed a smile. "Well cut, boy. Your woman is—is . . . at the grain shed."

Conan nodded. He acknowledged the information with the only thing he could think of that might repay the bleeding man. "You fought well, Brute."

The dying man closed his eyes, and nodded. Then he toppled forward and sprawled facedown in the street.

Conan slung the blood from his sword. The grain shed. He would find it, and the one who called himself the Disguise Master.

Sixteen

A hard rain began to fall. The clouds that had been piling up through the afternoon finally made good their threat, and the first assault consisted of hail, pea-sized and noisy.

Inside the grain shed, the musty smell lay over the coarse sacks full of barley, wheat, and rye, unabated by the rumble of hail upon the roof. The Disguise Master turned away from the spectacle of the store, as the forerunner to the rain proper ended. The white of the hail covering the ground gave way to its warmer brother, as the fat-drop rain began to pound.

Where was Brute? He was supposed to have been here, bearing the injured Conan, so that the Disguise Master could witness the final stroke.

One of the footpads cackled—he couldn't tell if it was Port or Starboard—and poked a finger at the captured woman, who sat bound and propped against a stack of grain bags.

"Cease that," the Disguise Master said almost absently.

The footpad looked up from his fingering, startled, and quickly withdrew his questing hand. "By your command, master."

161

The Disguise Master turned away, disgusted. To be reduced to working with such scum for more than a day or two rankled. The sooner this business was done, the better.

Where *was* that smelly assassin?

Neg could hardly control his hand as he reached for the Source of Light. Skeer held it out, still inside a leather bag, holding it by a drawstring as if he were loath to touch it any more than necessary.

"At last!" Neg said.

When he touched the bag, he felt a thrill run through his arm as might a current of hot fluid. He had not enjoyed such a sensation since the last time he had been with a woman, and that was many scores of years past.

Power. Power emanated from the talisman in raw waves, so much power that it bathed the room in its vibrations. Yes. Yes!

Neg tore his attention away from the device he held and looked at his agent. "My faithful servant, you have done all that I could expect. Your reward will be great."

He turned away from Skeer and moved to an oaken sideboard. He opened the cabinet and removed a cloth bag. Turning back toward Skeer, he spread the mouth of the bag so that the gold coins within caught the light and gleamed. He saw the greed in Skeer's glance, and smiled at it. He tossed the bag to his agent, who caught it deftly.

Neg returned to the sideboard and fetched a dusty bottle of wax-and-cork stoppered wine. "I have been saving this vintage for such a special occasion. Would you join me in a drink?"

Skeer smiled, hefting the gold. "Aye, master."

The necromancer nodded and cracked the seal on the wine. He produced two glasses and poured the liquid into them. The wine was the color of old rubies, and the sparkles in it reflected from Skeer's face as he raised his glass in a toast.

"To your goals," Skeer said.

"Aye," Neg said. "To my goals."

Skeer sniffed at the wine, took in the aroma, and tasted the red fluid. Excellent! He drained half the glass and smiled at Neg. His earlier fears, it seemed, had been entirely unjustified. The necromancer had been delighted, he had paid quickly and without demurring, and had even broken the seal on a bottle of very fine wine. What more could a man ask from a master?

He was nearing the end of his wine, when he began to feel somewhat dizzy.

"A problem?" Neg asked.

Skeer shook his head. "A touch of vertigo."

"Some more wine, perhaps?"

"N-no. I—I—"

Neg reached out, and Skeer thought the action was to steady him, but instead, the necromancer merely caught the wineglass in his fingers. "The glass is very expensive," he said. "I wouldn't want it to be broken when you fall."

Fall? What could he mean? Then he chanced to notice that Neg's own glass remained full, the wine untouched, and the realization fell upon him like an edge-weighted shroud: the wine, it must be—

"Poisoned," Neg said, as if catching his thought. "You served me so well in life, I should think you would serve even better in death."

Then the world went gray, and Skeer could not even summon the strength to curse as he fell. Before he hit the floor, oblivion claimed him, and Skeer no longer dwelled among the living.

Lightning flared over the gorge, and rain cascaded down the rocky walls, over mosses and lichens, drenching already-wet stone yet more. Thunder beat upon the sheer walls with loud fists, and the rain swirled on twisted winds, flying not only downward, but at odd angles seldom seen in flat lands.

On the west side of the gorge, six battered figures worked their way up the slick stone, ignoring winds, rain, lightning, and thunder. They were greatly spaced along the face of the rock, since some had fallen more than once, and had to begin the climb over. The farthest along had five or six spans left before he crested the gorge's lip, assuming he managed to maintain his grip for the remaining distance. The last in the ragged line of climbers had ten times that distance to traverse.

One of the climbers, the third in line, placed too much weight on a ledge of slick rock, and lost his footing and grasp upon the wall. He tumbled off, to fall silently to the rain-swelled river below. None of the other climbers spared him a glance. The five continued on doggedly, intent on the ascent.

As the third climber struck the water far below, another group of travelers reached the eastern edge of the gorge. What had been several thousand spiders was now reduced to only a few hundred, but their purpose, like the zombies before them, remained unabated. Without preamble, the spiders began to climb down the face of the gorge. Some fell almost immediately, others managed to cling to the wetness.

Overhead, the lightning spoke of the comic vision it saw

in the gorge, and its noisy child thunder laughed loudly at the joke.

Conan led Tuanne along a narrow alleyway. Here and there, overhanging roofs jutted out enough to block the main portion of the thunderstorm, but Conan spared the deluge little care. A man would not dissolve under a little rain, and Elashi was yet to be freed.

"There," Tuanne said, pointing through the rain. "That building is the grain shed. At least it was in my time."

Conan pulled his sword free of the lizard-skin sheath. He paused under the shelter of an overhang long enough to stone the edge where it had been nicked in the fight with Brute, but no longer. He started toward the shed.

"Will you not try and take them unawares?" Tuanne asked.

"I shall not skulk," Conan answered. "Direct action would be better here."

"Even if one of them holds a knife to her throat?"

He paused. "What you say has some merit," he admitted. "Have you an idea?"

"Aye. Allow me to enter. I can ascertain if Elashi is with them, and her position, and signal you if it is safe to attack."

"I would rather not send a woman in my stead," Conan said.

"You are most kind to be concerned, Conan." Her voice was very soft. "But they cannot harm me with their blades, in any event."

"Aye. I had forgotten."

"And that is the kindest comment anyone has made to me in a hundred years," she said, smiling. She raised herself onto her tiptoes and kissed him gently.

He watched her march across the rain-sodden ground toward the shed, and, as soon as she entered, strode after her. He flattened his back against the damp wood next to the door, and waited, his sword held ready.

"Conan!" he heard, and without hesitation, he leaped through the door.

Inside, Tuanne stood with a dagger buried in her breast, facing a rat-faced man who wore an expression of profound astonishment. Next to this man stood the one known as the Disguise Master; beyond, a third man scrambled for an exit on the far side of the building, while Elashi struggled to free herself from coils of thin rope binding her.

The Disguise Master produced a crossbow from somewhere, and swung it up to cover Conan. He triggered the quarrel, and the bolt sped forth, to impale the Cimmerian.

Once, in his childhood, Conan had seen a traveling troupe pass through his village. There were singers, dancers, and those who demonstrated more martial arts. Among the latter group was a thin, whippetlike man who performed a trick that had amazed all who saw it: he dodged arrows fired at him by bowmen. For weeks afterward, Conan and the other children of the village had practiced the trick, with the result usually being bruises caused by the blunt arrows shot from makeshift bows. Due to his quickness, Conan had been hit less often than most; the trick had been to move just at the instant the arrow left the bow. A half-second later was too late.

Even as Conan saw the crossbow come up, he started his shift. As a child, he had done the trick barehanded; now, however, he held a sword, and without thinking, he swung his weapon as he dodged. The short quarrel flew, and of a piece, Conan moved and cut—and sliced the wooden shaft in twain.

"By Set!" the Disguise master yelled, as the pieces of the quarrel tumbled and hit the far wall.

He was reaching for a second shaft as Conan leaped upon him, and bisected his head much as he had the arrow.

The rat-faced man turned to flee, following his faster comrade, and Conan took two steps to chase him, then stopped. Elashi was safe, that was the thing. Tuanne already moved to untie the desert girl. The Disguise Master wore his final earthly guise, and chasing two fleet footpads through the rain appealed little to Conan. He would be running merely to deal them justice, while they would be fleeing for their miserable hides. The gods who granted speed favored those who sprinted for life and limb more than they did those who would right wrongs. That was always the way of it.

Conan turned to Elashi. "Are you harmed?"

"What," began the woman, "took you so long?"

The Cimmerian youth could not suppress a grin. Unharmed she was.

Well. This place was as good as any to wait out the rain. After that, other problems faced them, not the least of which was figuring out a way into Neg's heavily defended castle.

Neg the Malefic had problems of his own. In the special chamber he had prepared, as pristine as a god's drinking glass, the Source of Light now nestled within the crystal carved to receive it. True, there had been a surge of energies when the talisman was so placed, but it was in no way operational at the level that he needed. Something had gone amiss, and he could not understand what.

His curses echoed from the walls as he raged back and

forth, trying to discern what portion of his spell was lacking. Damnation and Demons, what had he forgotten? It should work; he had done everything as the crumbling parchment directed, laid all the proper geas, spoken the incantations correctly—he was *certain* of it. Set knew he had practiced dozens of times while waiting for the talisman to arrive! What in all the gods-be-damned Hells was the matter?

Easy, Neg, he told himself. Do not upset yourself. Doubtless it is some simple step, something so minor it was overlooked. He would repeat the process, taking care to observe the smallest pronunciation correctly, the most minute detail. He had not done all this to fail over some niggling matter. He would have all the documents for the spells brought here, not trusting to his prodigious memory, and he would do it step by step until he had it right.

Neg turned to face the zombie who stood silently near the entrance, awaiting the necromancer's pleasure.

"Go to my library and fetch the *BiblioNecrum*, the *Book of the Damned*, and the *Black Folio*. Quickly."

Skeer, gazing back at his master through dull eyes, said, "By your command, lord." He turned and shambled off.

So close, Neg thought. He would not fail. No way.

The body that had been Skeer alive now functioned as well or better for Skeer dead; it did not, however, do so with Skeer in total command. True, he willed himself to actions—walking, standing, talking—but only by Neg's leave.

Such a state grated upon Skeer as nothing in his entire career had grated upon him. Rage which had smoldered and fueled for his entire life now burned hotly within his cold breast. To be treated this way, after all he had done for Neg! It rankled, it burned, it ate at his psyche like powerful acid upon soft flesh. Given his own control, he would slay Neg a thousand times, making each death worse than the one prior, delighting in each groan his victim made, finding ecstasy in every pained expression the necromancer could field. Ah, given his way . . .

There lay the problem, squarely in his ken. He had no such control. Neg's voice commanded, and he could not fail to obey; the thunder of a god's tongue could not do more to motivate Skeer than did Neg's softest whisper. He was in thrall to the wizard, and until he felt it, had never known the true meaning of that term.

He thought briefly, as he entered Neg's library, of the zombie woman he had drenched in saltwater. He understood, now, what it was she had wanted with the talisman. Some innate sense told him that the Source of Light was, for one cursed with reanimation as he now was, a key to the true death. A touch of the power the thing carried, and he would go to the Gray Lands.

And, he thought, as he dug a heavy book from the carved ebony cabinet, was that such a bad thing? True, to walk the earth, impervious to sword or poison, would be a thing of great power, in and of itself. Unfortunately, the drawbacks made the power worthless to one such as Skeer. The smoke of the hemp-weed did not bring visions to one without breath; neither did women hold any further interest for him in the ways he had known them before. Parts of him were more dead than others, so it seemed.

He found the second volume for which he had been sent, pulled it from its position next to a bookend made from a human skull and hammered brass, and continued his search for the final book. No, being a zombie meant being unable to enjoy those things for which he had spent his entire life working—and even if that had not been so, even if he *could* have those things, being in Neg's thrall prevented it in any case. Neg never released his nightwalkers. Some had been in his service for hundreds of years.

That such a fate lay in store for him Skeer did not doubt for an instant.

The third book came to light, and he retrieved it. Slowly, without the slightest joy, he began to trudge back toward the crystal chamber, bearing the leatherbound works for which he had been sent. Lapdog Skeer, he thought mirthlessly. For what crime did he deserve this? Certainly, he had offended as many gods as the next thief; the bodies of his victims, if piled up, would tower well over his head; he had despoiled women, stolen treasures, and done other things a reputable citizen would have nightmares about; still, others had done much worse, and they had not been condemned to this cruel fate!

From down the dusty corridor, Neg's voice echoed. "Hurry, damn you!"

So bidden, Skeer's legs took control, and he began to run. Inwardly, he cursed Neg, using every god of which he had ever heard.

It was, of course, to no avail.

All he could do was what Neg commanded. Do that, and wait, and hope something would happen.

Seventeen

"Aye," Conan said, "no doubt half the demons in Gehanna would willingly open a portal for you, Elashi. In this instance, however, I would prefer not to risk my neck on your sweet voice."

Elashi clenched her fists. "Just because we sleep together does not mean—"

"He is right," Tuanne cut in.

Elashi turned to face Tuanne. "You are taking *his* part?"

"Few men, if any, are as practiced in the arts of guile as Neg," Tuanne continued. "No one has ever tricked his way into the castle—not past the Men With No Eyes."

The three of them had returned to the inn, and sat alone in front of the fire, drying their clothes.

Tuanne said, "Conan's talents are many, as we both know, but trickery is not his forte."

Elashi nodded. "Aye. He is brutally honest, I must admit. One of his endearing characteristics—"

Conan grinned.

"—of which he has only a few," she finished.

Conan squeezed water from his left boot, then set it

closer to the fire, to dry. "I confess I cannot see an easy way into the castle. Alone, I might manage to bypass the moat beasts, scale the wall, and fight my way past the guards."

Tuanne shook her head. "The chances would be exceedingly slender. No one has ever done so before."

"Then what are our options?"

The zombie woman leaned toward the fire. Steam rose from her clothes, but she seemed unaffected by the heat.

"There is another way. There are dangers, perhaps as many as a direct assault on the castle itself."

Conan watched the shadows dance across her features as she spoke. She was an exceedingly beautiful woman.

"My contacts with the inhabitants of the Gray Lands over the years have given me access to certain knowledge. There is a way to travel in the In-Between Lands, and such travel covers territory in the real world at the same time."

Conan blinked. "I do not understand."

"Magic, Conan. A kind of shortcut."

The Cimmerian turned to stare into the fire. He did not enjoy talk of magic. Then again, he could think of no better way to achieve his goal at this point.

Outside, the rain continued unabated, tapping at the roof with liquid fingers. The sound lulled a listener, but Conan knew this was no time to feel relaxed. The hardest part of this entire venture seemed to lie ahead, and the path led through magic, making things yet worse.

The problem, Neg discovered, lay not in his pronunciation, but in his preparation. He had omitted a step: the crystal sconce upon which the Source of Light lay was spotlessly clean, but the instrument utilized to accomplish this deed had been the wrong one. He saw it now, and it was a natural enough mistake. Where he had translated the Kambujan word *wanitakala* to mean "clean woman," or virgin, it actually should have been *wanitakale*, whose meaning was altogether different. The "e" instead of "a" ending changed "clean" to "soiled," and instead of a virgin, he needed a trull. The ages had dimmed the manuscript and even the sharpest eye might have made the same mistake. Now that he looked for it, the word definitely ended differently than first he had thought.

So. He needed a brush made from the hair of a trull to dust the sconce. That done, the spell should proceed without problem.

"Skeer!"

The zombie appeared at the doorway.

"Go to the village and return with enough trull hair to make a brush this size." He held the hand-sized brush up. Then he tossed a pouch of coins at Skeer. "Pay whatever it takes, and hurry. I have no doubt you are well acquainted with all the whores of the village, so I expect you to return before night falls."

After Skeer had departed, Neg stood staring at the Source of Light. Such a small matter could interrupt the most complex magics. Well. It would be rectified before the day was gone. He could hardly wait.

Skeer felt the stares of the villagers burn into his back after he passed—none dared meet his gaze—and he felt something akin to shame. The rain had finally stopped, not that it bothered him, and he splashed through the standing puddles as he went to fetch that which he had been directed to collect. For the amount of gold in Neg's pouch, he could buy the hair of all the trulls in the village, and likely an arm or leg from each to go along with it. He would spend it all, to spite Neg, and cut only enough to fulfill the minimum requirements. Though he could no longer interact with women as he had before, the expression on Belinda's face—yes, she would do fine—would be interesting to behold.

That would be the extent of it, interest. All men had to die, Skeer knew that, even though he had never thought over much of his own end. Still, to be cut down in so dastardly a manner and by one for whom he had done such service . . . it still pained him more than he could begin to express. All he was missing, all he would miss—could there be a worse curse than to be faced with the things he wanted but could no longer enjoy? True Death was sweeter, and that denied him. Damn Neg to the depths of the deepest Hell!

But meanwhile, fetch the trull hair, as ordered, oh-so-obedient cur Skeer!

Determined spiders enspelled by the priests of a dark god moved faster than reanimated dead men, so it seemed. What had first been several thousand, then several hundred, now numbered only several dozen, but still they marched. Ordinarily much less sure of foot than a common window spider spinning its web in dusty eaves, the tarantulas made their way across waters and rocks, rain notwithstanding, and scuttled onward toward their goal.

Four of the things that had been men awaited at the edge of the gorge while their slower brothers finished the climb, and they took no notice of the spiders that crested the rocky lip and hurried westward.

The night began to settle upon the land, a darkening blanket laced with stars, but neither spiders nor zombies paid it heed, for neither spiders nor zombies lived for the joys of the light. It suited them, the night, for their purposes were darker than a Stygian pit, and in the surrender of sun to moon, they found, if not joy, at least a kind of unity of intent.

The spiders scuttled, and the zombies finished their climb and resumed their walk.

"It is him!" Elashi said.

Conan moved to the small and grimy window at which the desert woman stood, and peered out into the deepening shadows. The man who passed was none other than Skeer. Automatically, Conan's hand went to his sword's hilt. He felt Tuanne join them at the window, and further felt her start, stiffening at what she saw. He turned toward her.

"There is no need for that," she said, touching Conan's fingers on his sword's grip. "Skeer has become my brother in perversion."

"What do you mean?" Elashi said.

"He belongs to Neg even in death."

"A zombie?" the Cimmerian said.

"Aye. Neg's reward for a job accomplished."

Conan moved, as if to exit the inn.

"Where are you going?" Tuanne called.

"To speak with Skeer." He drew his blade.

"Do not! Your blade cannot kill him."

"He would move little without arms or legs," the Cimmerian said. "I shall carve him into slivers."

"Please, hold."

Conan paused. "You have no love for Skeer, dead or alive. Why do you ask this?"

"I have been Neg's creature for five times your lifespan. If Skeer sees you, he will likely guess I am nearby. If Neg knows where I am, he will . . . call to me. I cannot refuse his call, even though I managed to break away through his misuse of magicked salt before. I cannot bear the thought of falling back into Neg's thrall. Please.''

Conan rolled the sword in his palm, then resheathed the blade. "Aye. I suppose Skeer cannot help us at this point, in any event. And I would not have you distressed.''

Both women reached out to touch the Cimmerian's shoulders at the same moment. "Thank you,'' Tuanne said.

"And my thanks, as well,'' Elashi said.

The ingredients Tuanne needed for the spell to attain the In-Between Lands were, she said, simple. As the morning broke over the village, she, Elashi, and Conan went to the local market to obtain several items. Other things were not so easily located, but by noon, the zombie woman had all that she needed. Before she undertook to work the enchantment, she stopped to speak of the undertaking to her two friends.

"I have never been there,'' she said, "but the stories I have heard are frightening. While we have day here, it might be night there. There will be a road, as part of the spell, to lead us to the interior of Neg's castle; to leave this road is to court disaster. Even upon the path, safety can easily be imperiled, by all manner of unnatural creatures. Even accomplished witches or wizards tread very carefully in the In-Between Lands, and we shall have no such protections as they. I do not think I can be given the true death, even there, but certainly you could, and what might happen to me could be worse. You must know these things ere we attempt this journey.''

Elashi glanced at Conan, then back at Tuanne. "My

father walks the Gray Lands unavenged,'' she said, ''and I will do whatever is needed to end that shame.''

''Get on with it,'' Conan said. ''Where any mortal may walk, Conan does not fear to tread.''

''Very well. Stand near me.''

She began to chant, a strange, singsong melody, and while doing so, she lit a brazier that quickly filled the rented room with a spicy, aromatic smoke. The small fire in the metal pot seemed normal enough, until Tuanne tossed several items into it, changing the flame from red-orange to green, and then a blue to rival the summer skies over Cimmeria. Conan's vision began to play tricks on him, as the walls seemed to waver and bend, leaving no straight lines.

At the door, the innkeep knocked. ''Are you cooking something in there? We do not allow cooking or sacrifices in the rooms!''

''Ignore him,'' Tuanne ordered.

The knock grew louder. ''Hey! Within! I smell something burning! Is that goat flesh roasting?''

''Begone!'' Conan ordered. ''Else it be human flesh charring, and yours to boot!''

The knocking ceased abruptly, and the sound of hasty footsteps retreating reached Conan's ears. He allowed himself a small smile.

The smoke from the brazier now seemed to fill the room; the Cimmerian could not even see the walls. Suddenly, he felt a draft, as though the window had been opened, and the smoke began to clear.

When the vapors had thinned enough, what Conan saw was no longer the inside of a second-rate inn in some small village; rather, he stood on a plateau, part of a vast plain, and the air swam with tiny motes under a blue-green sun.

He swallowed, and looked around, his hand going instinctively to his sword. To the west—if that direction was west here—lay a vast jungle. To the east, what seemed an endless desert. Northward was a sea—if any body of water had ever been the color of fresh blood—and to the south, a range of mountains that must hold up the very sky, so tall were they. He looked down, to see a narrow path beneath his feet, leading down the plateau toward the distant jungle. It was the only road in sight, and nothing stood upon it save the three of them.

Conan turned to Tuanne with the question unspoken but apparent.

She nodded. "We are here."

Elashi pointed at the jungle, the strange light making her skin an eerie blue several shades darker than the pale blue of Tuanne's skin. "Is that where we are to go?"

Tuanne nodded again. "Aye. That jungle represents Neg's castle. If we survive to attain the middle of it, we shall find ourselves past his perimeter in the real world.

"If we survive. . . ."

Eighteen

With a set of fine steel shears, Neg trimmed the last of the
stray hairs from the new brush. A blonde, not that it
mattered, and hair as fine and soft as a baby's. It could
have just as easily been as coarse as a pig's back, for all he
cared, as long as it worked.

The Source of Light nestled in its bag hung from his
belt, bumping gently against his hip as he lifted the whore's-
hair brush and began to gently dust the already-spotless
crystal. He would have hurried, but such spells were, as he
had already been made all too aware, fragile. Meticu-
lously, he covered every part of the carved mineral with
the fine brush, cleaning invisible particles away. Too small
to see, they might be, but large enough to foul the spell,
that much he knew.

He spent perhaps ten minutes going over the crystal
before he decided he had done enough. He took a deep
breath, allowed it freedom, then placed the brush in his
pouch as he removed the talisman.

So softly did he place the Source of Light into the niche

for it that it would not have disturbed the slumber of a mouse.

There. Done. Now, to finish the incantations and see if his work had been successful.

His voice held the proper tones as he chanted the magic words, but there lay within them an additional fire now, a force he could feel. It was different from before, no doubt. It was going to work, he was sure of it!

When he was done, there could be no doubt of it. The Source of Light began to glow, pulsing as if alive, giving off a radiant light of such clarity that it hurt his eyes to gaze upon it. Power surged forth, power compared to which the earlier force he had felt was as nothing.

It began to fill him, that power, as wine filled an empty vessel, splashing within and against his walls, lighting a magic pyre upon every atom of his being.

Power! To mold as he chose! And his way was life and death, one unto the other. The energies boiled within his black soul, and he knew, he *knew* he could give or take life with a glance! As long as the talisman lay safely within its crystal receptacle, he, Neg the Malefic, would be Neg the Omnipotent!

He strode out into the hall. "Attend!" he said, his voice like thunder. Immediately, a dozen of the Men With No Eyes appeared.

"Guard this door," he ordered. "No one is to enter except me."

The blind priests scurried to obey. All save one.

"You," Neg said. "Look at me."

The man turned his sightless eyes toward the necromancer.

"Die," Neg said. He stared hard at the priest.

The man toppled soundlessly, until he hit the flagstones. Dead, and no doubt.

Neg smiled at his handiwork. "Live," he said, waving his hand toward the dead man.

Wordlessly, the priest lifted his head, then got back to his feet.

Neg laughed. Power! "Stay with the others," he said. The now-zombie priest moved away.

Neg turned, his cape flaring dramatically, and strode off down the hallway. He had done it! He would begin to raise his army immediately. Within a fortnight, the world would tremble before the might of Neg!

His laugh echoed along the stone walls.

Within their catacombs, the rats crouched lower, suddenly afraid.

The descent from the plateau was easy enough, although the shifting light, now blue, now red, now almost normal, played hob with the footing at times. Conan led, Elashi followed, and Tuanne brought up the rear. Thus far, they had seen no signs of life, and just as well, as far as Conan was concerned. To the north, the sea of blood danced under the colors, red, purple, nearly black, and back again. The jungle lay ahead.

Earlier, the Cimmerian had voiced his concern that the jungle stood much farther away than Neg's castle did from the village. Tuanne had answered that there was no direct correlation between distances in the real world and the In-Between Lands. A mile in one could be a foot in the other, and no way to tell which way it would translate.

Very well. Whatever it required, he would do. At times, he doubted his wisdom in pursuing this whole affair; still, a friend, albeit one of short duration, had died. Someone owed for that, and Conan of Cimmeria did not shirk his duty, no matter what the obstacles.

A wind began to blow from the desert behind them, hot and dry, offering to parch instead of cool. Dust devils sprouted ahead, swirling brown and full of dead, dry topsoil. There were two, no, three—*hist!* what was this?

The dust devils coalesced, compacting, growing opaque and dark. As they shrank in size, they sharpened in character, so that after a moment, what moved ahead was no longer air but solid, walking on two legs upright as did men. But no form of men were these creatures, least none of which Conan had seen or heard.

The things moved toward the human trio, and as they grew closer, Conan saw that they bore a resemblance to birds: where a man's face would be, a raptor's beak protruded from what was undeniably feathers. Large orange eyes shifted in the feathery masks; shoulders sloped to short but vestigial wings, the ends of which were hooked into obsidian-colored claws, three on each wing. The legs looked manlike, but the feet were high-arched and clawed as the wings.

Conan unlimbered his sword, swinging it back and forth to loosen the muscles of his shoulders, shifting his grip as might a man tuning a flute, until he found the proper position.

"Can we go around them?" Elashi said from behind him.

"To step from the road might conjure worse," Tuanne answered. "We could go back and hope they might not follow."

"Nay," Conan said, "our path leads that way, and they will allow us to pass—one way or another." This was a threat he could deal with, win or lose.

"Then allow me to lead," Tuanne said. "My flesh is repellent to beasts, and not liable to damage as is yours."

"Nay, again," Conan said. "No one holds Elashi at knifepoint here."

"You should at least try to reason with them," Elashi said. "Perhaps they mean us no harm."

When the strange birds were less than three spans away, Conan raised his sword and aimed its point at the eyes of the leading one. "Ho, feathered ones! Allow us to pass in peace."

The leader, whose feathers gleamed a darker blue-black than the other two giant avians, opened his hooked bill and emitted a piercing *craw!* but slowed not his advance.

"So much for reason," Conan said to Elashi. "You cannot say I did not try."

Two spans from the Cimmerian, the leader of the small flock leaped, and his jump carried him twice Conan's height into the dry air. He flapped his wings, and the rustle filled Conan's ears. He did not fly well, the big bird, but he had enough power to outhop any human athlete.

The move caught Conan by surprise, and the Cimmerian twisted to follow the short flight with his blade, only to feel the sting of the thing's foot claws on his shoulder as the creature dipped suddenly and slashed at him. Cimmerian blood ran down a muscular arm, but the wound was shallow and nearly painless.

The birdman touched down and bounced lightly into the air again.

Behind him, Conan heard the flutter of more wings, and he spun to face the other two avian monsters. Both of them took to the air as had the leader, but this time, the Cimmerian youth was prepared for the motion. He leaped, nearly half

his own height into the air, and slashed with his heavy
sword. The tip of the weapon scored, digging a deep
furrow into the right leg of one of the birdmen. The thing
squawked loudly, and rained scarlet from the wound.

Conan grinned as he twisted to face the beasts again.
Magical they might be, but they could bleed well enough.

The wounded birdman touched down, and collapsed into
a heap. Surely the injury was not so great . . .

As he watched, the stricken bird dissolved into a spinning wind, becoming once again a small dust devil that
quickly scattered, spraying sand over the combatants. Conan
blinked against the dust, and swung his sword to ward off
a second attack from the leader. Both missed their marks.

"The touch of iron is fatal," Tuanne said. "It is so with
many magical beings."

"Good," Conan said.

The two remaining creatures began to synchronize their
attacks, though, one darting in while the Cimmerian turned
to hack at the second. They were very fast, these birdmen.

As Conan whipped around to face the leader again, he
heard a startled squawk from the one behind him, then the
sound of a body thumping into the dirt. When the leader
dodged and leaped that way, the Cimmerian youth saw the
other birdman lying on the ground, Elashi's dagger sunk in
one lower leg. He grinned.

As the wind began again, swirling dust into his face, the
leader of the birdmen attacked.

"*Skreee!*" it screeched as it dropped for Conan, all its
claws extended.

The man leaped to his left and swung his sword. Feathers flew as the edge sliced into the thing's chest and tore
completely through it. It must be almost hollow, Conan

thought, as the leader of the attackers flopped onto the ground.

After the wind died, the three travelers looked at each other. Both women made a fuss over Conan's wound. In truth, it was hardly more than a scratch; still, he did not object to their ministrations. He said, "If that is the worst we have to face on this journey, it will be no hardship."

"Unfortunately, that might well be the least of our worries," Tuanne said. "I have heard tales that would make these beasts seem like sparrows."

"Spare me the tales," Conan said. "Some things are better left unspoken."

The three started along the path again.

The denizens of Neg's moat had an unexpected feeding, as dozens of fat, juicy spiders began to leap into the water, swimming for the castle. The feast did not last long, however, as the taste of the ensorcelled arachnids lay exceedingly foul upon the palates of the submarine guards. Whether it was the natural flavor of tarantula or some vouchsafe bitterness added by magic mattered not to the fishes of the circle; the unspoken word passed among them rapidly: *pauugh!* Eat not the black crawlies, they taste *bad* in the extreme!

So it was that some two dozen of the hardiest tarantula reached the base of Neg's castle. Following rat burrows and mole paths, they continued onward, gaining entrance to the home of the one they sought. He called to them, the accursed one did, and they went to fulfill their destiny, as messengers of an angry god.

Skeer trudged along, bearing a bowl of fruit for his

majesty Neg's diet, when he saw the spiders. So startled was he that he dropped the wooden bowl, scattering grapes, dates, and plums over the floor in a shower. The bowl clattered loudly on the gray flagstones.

"What is that racket?" Neg called.

Skeer, petrified, could not summon an answer.

The spiders scurried for the zombie, close to their goal at last.

Neg entered the hallway. "Skeer, what clumsiness have you discovered—?" He stopped, and looked at the spiders. "Ho, friends of yours, be these?"

"Th-th-they began following me in the c-c-city of Opkothard, Master!"

"Ah. The Shes. I have heard of the curse. They are ensorcelled, sent to kill you. You must have offended the local priests somehow. Came a long way, they did."

"M-m-master, can you not help me?"

Neg laughed, long and hard.

The spiders drew nearer, and Skeer stood as if rooted to the floor.

"M-master?"

"Fool! You are *dead*! What harm can these do to you now?"

Abruptly, Skeer knew the truth of it. He *was* dead!

"Fetch me another bowl of fruit, lout." Neg turned and swept out of the hall.

The first spider reached Skeer's leg. Its touch bothered him, but when it sank its fangs into his calf, it was no more bothersome than a mosquito bite would have been when he was alive. He reached down to crush the spider, then merely brushed it away. What would it do?

The spider scuttled back a few feet, and was surrounded

by its fellows, who stopped. It seemed somehow to be communicating.

Skeer turned, first picking up the overturned fruit bowl, and started back toward the kitchen. The spiders followed. He stopped.

They stopped.

He took two steps.

The tarantulas scuttled along.

He stopped again.

The spiders froze.

Skeer laughed. How frustrating it must be to find their quarry dead but still moving. What was an ensorcelled creature to do? Biting Skeer was a waste of venom, perhaps that was what the one had told the others. So now, their purpose blocked, where should they go? Apparently, they had decided to follow Skeer, lacking any other purpose. Like so many dogs, following him.

Skeer started back toward the kitchen, and his eight-legged retinue followed, keeping a span of distance between him and themselves. He laughed again. Odd how things turned out. Who would have thought a few weeks ago that he would be dead, enthralled as a zombie, and lord of perhaps thirty-odd fat and furry spiders? Good that he was not a storyteller or minstrel—no one would believe such a tale. It was too fanciful for words or song.

He went to attend to his master's chore, followed by his wiggling, furry carpet.

.

At the inn, six dead men crowded into the empty room. They looked at the brazier in silence, smelled the magical herbs and spices in silence, and realized where their quarry had gone, again without audible sound.

Two of the zombies left, to gather ingredients. The

others awaited their return. Leaving the world for magic lands might have gained their quarry time, but it bought them little else—the Men With No Eyes would not be deterred by such a tactic.

Later, when the smoke cleared, the small room at the inn once again stood empty, and the innkeep shuddered as he wondered how so many people had gone in and none had come out.

Nineteen

The Opkothardian morgue attendant had recovered from his fright, though he would swear there were gray hairs on his head and in his beard that had not been there before. Seeing six dead men rise and walk again certainly was enough to take several years off any sane man's life.

Of course, he thought, as he leaned against the cool wall of the morgue, staring at this latest batch of charges, those six had been unusual. Outlanders, and dead by violence, so who knew what evil lurked in their souls? All the corpses currently occupying his vault were, thank the Nameless, local people, and dead of natural causes, for the most part: a jar of bad figs laid one family of four down, the red fever took several more, a collapsed wall gave him three workers who were slower to move than others. And one very old man had simply removed his clothes and laid down in the public baths to be fished out several hours later when someone noticed he had not surfaced. Little chance for evil doings in this lot.

He was calm enough, then, when he heard the rat skittering in the back among the far tables. Rats he could deal with.

He picked up the dart he had had Zenk the knifemaker construct for him. This item consisted of a length of wood a few inches long with a sharpened nail sticking from one end and stabilizing feathers on the other. It looked like a short and squat arrow, but it was accurate when thrown at close range, and he had lately skewered many an unsuspecting rodent with it. He grinned as he slowly made his way back toward the dark corner.

The grin faded abruptly when he saw the wrinkled corpse of the drowned old man sit up suddenly. The only thing he could think to do in his terror was to toss the dart. The small weapon stuck in the old man's shoulder, but if it bothered the corpse, it did not show.

Then the others began to stir. All around him, the dead rose from their slabs, not speaking, but moving as though alive otherwise.

The morgue attendant ran screaming from the room. The only way he would ever enter it again, he swore, was when somebody carried his lifeless body inside!

Nearing the In-Between Lands, Tuanne stopped suddenly, and seemed to sway as if she might fall. Conan said, "Are you all right?"

"It's Neg," she said, eyes closed. "He has begun to use the power of the talisman. He calls to the dead."

Conan and Elashi looked around. They were alone.

"I can feel it pull at me," Tuanne continued. "It is a strong call. A command."

"Can you resist it?" Elashi asked.

"For now. Do you have the salt I gave you?"

Conan looked at the woman from the desert. He knew not of this.

Elashi said, "I have it."

"If I should falter, you must use it. If Neg's power grows, I will have to go to him. By a different path than that upon which we now tread."

"But the dangers—"

"It will not matter. I will have to obey."

"Then let us hurry," Conan said. "The sooner we arrive and dispatch this cursed man, the better."

As the "day" wore on, Conan began to see the effects of Neg's sorcery. In the distance, figures appeared, walking at right angles to the path upon which the trio traveled. When these grew nearer, Conan reached for his sword.

"Nay," Tuanne said. "They will not harm us. Look at them."

They were people right enough, Conan saw. But what the blue fire of his eyes reflected upon were people in thrall. Men, women, children, marching across their path, unaware of Conan and his companions. They seemed to be sleepwalkers, looking straight ahead, as if drawn by some invisible string.

"The souls of the dead who have yet to make the final passage into the Gray Lands," Tuanne said. "They are called back to their bodies by the power of Neg's weird.

"Most are recently dead; some, likely, have been in the ground longer, but had passage delayed for some reason. Those bodies will not be pleasant to look upon when their former owners return."

"Ugh," Elashi said.

Conan did not speak to this, but his reaction paralleled Elashi's. A corpse more than a few days moldering, even in winter, was not an appetizing sight.

The numbers of the crosswalkers grew as the three neared the jungle; hundreds, mayhaps thousands of them had passed and there seemed to be no end to them.

"Within a few days Neg will have an army surrounding his castle," Tuanne said. "All the dead for a thousand miles will flock to him. No one not in his command will be able to even approach his stronghold. No one alive."

Tuanne swayed again, and stopped walking. She started to walk after the latest group moving aslant to them.

"Tuanne!" Elashi called.

The zombie woman took another step, then stopped. She shook her head, turned to look at her companion, then quickly stepped back onto the path. "His power increases," she said.

Conan saw that Elashi held cupped in her palm a measure of salt crystals. She returned them to her purse and dusted her hand.

"We shall arrive at the edge of the jungle in an hour, I judge," Conan said. "Come."

The armies of the night were stirring.

In his highest chamber, Neg looked through the window out into his domain—it was *all* his domain now!—at the figures in the distance. They came. From all directions, as far as Neg's eye could discern, they came.

He laughed, deep and booming, and waved to those who could not see him but who felt his call. Come to me, he thought, come and join the most powerful force ever assembled. An unkillable, unstoppable force, commanded by me. Come!

The power flowed through him stronger now, as he grew more used to the workings of it. It streamed away from him as light streamed from the sun. He was god to all the dead, and they were his worshippers, come to bow to him.

The armies of the night stirred, and came to their master.

*   *   *

Surprise was too mild a term for what the Disguise Master felt. He should be dead, no man could live after such a stroke as the barbarian had delivered with his heavy blade. He recalled it vividly: as his entire life sped by, the gods-be-cursed Conan had chopped down, and—

The Disguise Master reached up and felt his head.

There lay down the middle of his skull a gap, half the width of his finger, narrowing by the time it reached a spot between his eyes in the front, and the crown in the back. Inside the gap he felt a squishy softness—his brain, he did not doubt—and at that instant the Disguise Master very nearly went mad. No man could live with such a wound!

It was then that he realized that he was not breathing.

He could draw in a breath, true enough, but it did not seem to matter if he held or released it. Experimentally, he spoke, and that worked well enough, if he remembered to pull in enough air to work his voice.

Realization dawned at the same instant that he felt compelled to start walking.

He was dead.

Dead he was, but brought back somehow. Therefore, he must be a zombie. And, likely it was Neg who commanded his feet to move. The unnaturalness of it filled him with dread, but then there came an ameliorating thought: perhaps he might have a second chance at slaying Conan, did he still live.

The smile that crossed the Disguise Master's face twisted his lips in a cruel sneer as he thought of that possibility. Perhaps the gods were not to be cursed after all.

As he moved down the road for he knew not where, he saw others moving as he did. There was Brute, sans one arm, plodding along. Others he did not recognize, many of them. This Neg had power, no doubt of that. Well. He would see what he would see. Meanwhile, he would content himself with the thought of meeting Conan again. This time, should it happen, he would have an advantage: a dead man could not be slain.

Across the land they rose.

Malo, who had been a Suddah Oblate, stood and shuffled to the west. Behind him, two of his brother priests also found themselves alive but not alive.

A nightwatchman who had been careless dug his way through still-damp earth and joined the parade of dead.

Two mountain bandits who had been ambitious but unskilled drew what the beasts had left of them together and started down the mountain.

Across the land, they rose. The gutter scum of Shadizar; the hanged footpads of Numalia; the sacrificed of black Stygian rites; the good, the evil, the criminal, and the blameless. All who had died within a thousand miles of Neg's castle, all who had not yet been awarded a permanent place in the Gray Lands, all who had limbs enough to walk or to crawl, all of them rose, from biers, from sepulchers, from coffins, from unmarked graves. Rose, they did, and went to meet their new master.

The armies of the night marched.

Night fell suddenly in the In-Between Lands. Dusk laid the softest of hands on the road, and then night fell almost as quickly as a lamp deprived of fat.

The jungle edge lay five minutes away, but Conan had no desire to attempt that entrance in the dark.

"We camp here," he said. No one disagreed.

He journeyed to the nearest copse to obtain firewood.

He did not know if the creatures that inhabited this world would fear fire, but fear it or not, a flaming brand shoved into one's face would give one pause in any event.

They ate dried strips of fruit and smoked fish that Elashi had packed in her purse. Conan washed the distasteful stuff down with small sips of wine he had thought to bring in a leather bottle. He drank sparingly—a man would not want his wits dulled here—and wondered if the fire might draw unwanted attention. Upon reconsideration, he decided that he would find a sheltered spot away from the fire, the better to see the surrounding territory, and anything that might find its way to the light.

Overhead, there were stars, but no moon. The sky bore no resemblance to any he had ever seen: the familiar constellations did not shine here. Here, he saw a curve of points that seemed like a knife blade; an irregular ring that lay low on the horizon; a thick collection of hard diamonds that almost seemed like a man's fist. Had there been any doubt that the land he walked was other than his world, this sky would certainly have dispelled it.

After the meal Conan added wood to the fire. "Let us move away from the fire," he said. "So that anything curious about it will not happen upon us unawares."

Again, neither woman demurred, and they found a ring of scrubby bushes half a minute's walk from the fire. He considered sitting watch, but since Tuanne did not sleep, decided that his time would be better spent in rest. Her eyes were better suited to the dark than his, and she could awaken him if danger threatened.

With Elashi on one side and Tuanne on the other, Conan drifted into a deep and tired slumber.

He awoke to see that Tuanne was gone.

False dawn lay over the In-Between Lands. The fire had burned down to a few glowing coals and leaving the path had drawn no new terrors, but Tuanne was nowhere in sight.

He sat up, and Elashi awoke.

"What is it?"

"Tuanne is gone," he said.

They scrambled to their feet and left the cover of the brush, but the darkness was impenetrable beyond a few spans.

"We must find her!" Elashi said.

"It is too dark," Conan replied. "We would only lose the path ourselves."

"We cannot leave her here!"

"I am open to suggestion."

Elashi fell silent.

"She said her path would differ from ours, if she succumbed to Neg's call," Conan said. "We must get to Neg's castle; that is our best hope of saving her."

"How will we get out of this place?" Elashi asked, voicing Conan's own worry. "I do not know the spell, nor do you."

"She said this path was built especially for us. Perhaps there will be some indication when we reach the proper point."

"And perhaps we shall wander around in this place until our bones turn to dust!"

"I am open to suggest—"

"Stop saying that!"

The first rays of the strange dawn began to light the dark sky, and Conan kept his words within. There was nothing else to be done. He could understand her fear.

Better she should say it than he.

*   *   *

The novelty of being followed by his own small hirsute army soon palled for Skeer. They followed him everywhere. Since he was spared sleep and elimination, he did not have to worry about awakening to a spidery blanket, or treading on one in the confines of an outhouse; still, they never left him.

In a fit of pique, Skeer decided to eliminate the damned things. He lunged across the small distance separating the tarantulas from himself. Almost as if they anticipated his move, the furry-legged creatures scattered. As fast as he could move, he only managed to catch one of them under his sandaled foot. It gave out a satisfying *crunch!* and splattered arachnidal gore in a spokelike pattern, but try as he did, he could not catch any of the others. He was certain that their speed was not natural, so fast did they skitter away. Were he alive, he would have exhausted himself trying to kill the things. As it was, he eventually realized the futility of his efforts, despite his lack of anything better to do.

As soon as he ceased trying to mash the life from them, the spiders regrouped. Twenty-two of the little bastards, he counted. Life had had its bad moments; death, it seemed, was ever so much worse.

Skeer walked the empty halls of Neg's castle, stirring seldom-trod dust and thinking black thoughts.

Tuanne knew she was lost. The touch of Neg's mind was but fleeting upon her, other than the same compunction that drew the others walking the In-Between Lands, but with that touch she knew he had seen her.

Ah, Tuanne! I thought you might return. I have several new pleasures in mind for you upon your arrival. You

*departed without bidding me so much as a simple farewell.
I am injured.*

Neg's mental voice hardened, the crack of a psychic
whip. *I am injured; so shall you be. . . .*

With that, Tuanne's hopes dwindled to a pinpoint, buried under resignation so heavy that a mountain seemed
light by comparison. To be Neg's slave for a thousand
years, the object of his ire for once escaping, loomed over
her blacker than the darkest cave under any heaven.

Along with souls of the others ensnared in his curse,
Tuanne continued to walk.

There was no longer any need for the village that had
sustained him for centuries. As a test of his power, Neg
sent a wave of his new troops into the hamlet.

Those villagers who did not flee shortly became part of
his new army.

As the evening deepened to violet and then black, the
flames of the burning village made a nice light to view the
several thousand zombies who gathered outside his moat.

"Speak my name!" he commanded.

With one voice, they spoke. Because some were farther
away than others, the sound swelled and droned into a roar
like a breaking wave upon a beach.

"Neg! Neg! Neg!"

His chest swelled with power and pride.

"NEG! NEG! NEG!"

"NEG-NEG-NEG-NEG-NEG-NEG-NEG-NEG . . ."

Yes. Neg. Master of the world.

Twenty

The jungle steamed around them, deep green, and the light that filtered through the thick canopy above seemed as normal as that of the land to which they journeyed. No longer blue, the sun, when he glimpsed it, burned yellow and hot. Conan's sweat attested to the heat. Next to him, Elashi removed her outer garments, to tie them around her shapely hips.

It was an odd jungle. No insects swarmed the air, no sounds of beasts hunting in the distance reached their ears. For all the dangers that Tuanne had warned them of, nothing came to interrupt their journey.

Two hours walk into the sodden bush, and they came to the end of their quest in the magic lands.

"You were right," Elashi admitted. "That must be how we are to reenter our own world."

Ahead lay what appeared to be the grandfather of all trees; on its side, a wooden gate hung, twice the height of a man. Standing guard over this portal was a large and muscular man holding a sword, clad only in a loincloth and boots.

The man looked familiar. He was easily as large as Conan, had square-cut black hair to his shoulders, and stood with a kind of arrogance.

Crom! It could not be!

"By Mitra!" Elashi said. "It—it is—is—"

"Myself," Conan finished.

"It cannot be."

"A fair copy, then. Although methinks he looks too insolent."

Elashi said, "Oh, no, he is the exact image of you."

Conan looked at her. "You should get along as well with him as you do with me, then." His voice was very dry.

"I think not," she replied, pointing.

The ersatz Conan stalked toward them.

"Ho," the real Conan said.

The copy stopped and looked puzzled. One might say almost stupidly so, Conan thought, then shook that idea away. Natural wonderment.

"What do you want?" the fake Cimmerian said.

"To pass yon gate," Conan replied.

"You may not. I am charged with preventing any entry."

"Does this include yourself?"

"Nay. But," the fake continued, "you are not me. You are some demonish illusion. Magic!" He spat.

Conan resisted the urge to expectorate in agreement. Instead, he said, "It is you who are the illusion. Let us pass, and you may continue to wear my form."

"Nay, demon. And I shall see *your* true shape after I cut away your magical veil." So saying, the gate guard drew his sword and took a stance.

Conan's grin was wolfish as he replied with his own blade, matching the other's stand. He strode forward, raised his weapon, and cut at the other's head, hard.

The block offered could not have been better placed; more, it carried every bit as much power as Conan's strike. A bad sign.

The counterfeit Conan looked surprised again.

Surely, the genuine Conan thought, surely I do not offer such an expression to the world? I must find a looking glass someday.

Not now, however, he thought, as the fake slashed at his arm. Conan danced back and parried, then circled the move into a stab at the thick chest. The imitation leaped back fleetly, and the strike fell well short.

Two more minutes of thrust and counterthrust ended in a draw, neither man having touched the other. How could a man defeat himself? Conan worried the thought as he feinted a broad sweep and bore in for a short cut to the neck. His move was anticipated, blocked handily, and in a comic touch to the already comic proceedings, then duplicated exactly by the false Conan. As was Conan's next block.

"Crom!" both men said at the same instant.

"Perhaps you can reason with him," Elashi offered as the paired Conans stood facing each other two spans away.

"Reason? You jest," the real Conan said.

The other Conan laughed.

Then again, who better to reason with than yourself?

The genuine Cimmerian—although he wondered if perhaps the other man might not think *he* was the real article too—lowered his blade.

"If one of us is a fake, he is a good one," Conan said.

The tree gate guardian nodded. "I'll allow that."

"But what if we are both real?"

"Unlikely."

"Granted, but possible in this land of magic, you must agree."

"Aye. Possible."

"Then if that is true, to allow me to pass through the gate would be no dereliction of your duty."

Grudgingly, the other nodded. "True enough."

"Then allow me to pass, for I *know* I am real."

The ersatz Conan pondered upon that for a moment. "Even if what you say is true, what about her?"

Conan was stumped for a reply.

Elashi said, "I? I am merely an illusion."

"An illusion?"

"Aye. A phantom. Not real. A ghost."

"Hmm. Were that the case, you could pass. But I would have to determine the truth of it."

Elashi smiled. "Easily done. Touch me. Your hand will pass through unimpeded."

The real Conan stared at her. Had she gone mad? She was no illusion! *His* hand had never passed through her warm flesh!

Elashi took a step forward, turned her head slightly, and winked at the real Conan.

Ah. Now he understood. "Yes, touch her," he said, sheathing his sword.

The fake Conan lowered his blade, now that the threat seemed to be gone. He took two steps toward Elashi.

She chose that moment to lift her thin undershirt, baring her full and tanned breasts. "Here," she said. "Feel."

When the copy Conan extended his hand to stroke those perfect globes, the real Conan leaped, and clouted the other behind the ear with a powerful hammerblow of his knotted fist. The fake Conan dropped, his consciousness knocked from him.

Elashi grinned, and covered herself.

"I would not have been duped that way," Conan said.

Her grin grew larger.

"I would not have," Conan insisted.

"Of course not," she said. But she did not stop smiling.

As they moved to the gate, the vision of the half-naked Elashi as she had stood there lay heavily upon his memory. He could hardly blame the other Conan, who sprawled sleeping on the soggy ground. It was a fine sight, truly it was. Not that he would have fallen for such a trick. Really.

Neg discovered yet another trick given him by his new powers. He could, if he so desired, "see" through the eyes of a designated zombie. It required merely his willing this after making mental contact, and he became instantly able to be in two places at once, one fully and the other in a kind of dreamlike state. Depending upon his intent, the "real" sight could be either place. More, he could shift his mind into the bodies of the Men With No Eyes, and that proved to be most interesting. Though blind, their other senses were so acute so as to render the sightless state only a minor annoyance. He tried the technique on one of the living villagers brought to him as a test subject, but could not make the shift. Ah, well. A small matter. Upon the quick death of the villager, the deed became possible.

Soon, his army would be large enough to send sweeping all before it. He merely needed to decide upon a direction. Should he go north, into Corinthia, Nemedia, and Brythunia? Or perhaps farther west, taking Ophir and Aquilonia, to the sea state of Zingara? Koth and Shem lay southward, and beyond them Stygia and Kush, and to the east, Zamora and Turan. . . .

Ah, such decisions! Not that it mattered which way he

chose to conquer first; in the end, it would all be his. With each battle, his army would grow; every fallen soldier would become his man, every civilian slain another. The greater the defenses, the faster his forces would grow. An invincible army of dead, never needing sleep or food or rest, would sweep all before it, as a wind moved dry leaves.

Then, once he ruled the entire world, he could do anything. Anything! He would rule for ten thousand years!

The last man alive in a world filled with dead servants.

The door though the tree led to a dark corridor. Conan led, his sword probing ahead, while Elashi clutched onto his belt from behind.

After a moment, they saw a dim light ahead.

Another moment, and the light proved to be a guttering fat lamp on the wall of a quite ordinary stone corridor. Conan felt a coldness as he passed through the portal into the necromancer's castle. When he turned to look at the exit, he saw nothing but a blank stone wall.

"Are we here?" Elashi said.

"So it would seem."

"Now what?"

"Now we find Neg and kill him."

Five zombies walked through the In-Between Lands as a unit, five who had been Men With No Eyes. The sixth now rested, if somewhat uncomfortably, within the bowels of a creature the size of a terrestial whale. This monster had burrowed up through the road on which the six traveled and engulfed the zombie in a single bite. If the taste of dead flesh reanimated bothered the creature, it gave no sign, but sank back into the land as if it were water, and disappeared, bearing its most recent dinner with it.

The five continued on without their colleague.

Unbeknownst to Elashi and Conan, Tuanne had taken the same route into Neg's castle, albeit before the counterfeit Conan arrived to take up his post. It was to this portal that the five remaining trackers unerringly moved.

At the giant tree they met the false Conan.

"I have been tricked once," he said. "It will not happen again. Leave."

The zombie priests had no such intentions. They started toward the gate.

Whichever god or demigod who had duplicated Conan, whatever his, her, or its reasons, had done an exceedingly good job. The rage that smoldered and flared within the construct erupted like a human volcano. He flew into the five priests, sword blurring back and forth, up and down, this way and that, and abruptly, the air was filled with a rain of dead flesh. Hands, arms, feet, ears, a head— everything the cold sharp iron could find it severed and flung hither and yon. Some of the more mobile pieces— hands, especially—tried to return to their owners, scrabbling along like fleshy insects, but the flashing blade never let up long enough to allow it.

Even the rage of a fake Cimmerian is an awesome sight.

When the man finally exhausted even his great strength, the clearing by the giant tree lay deep in bloodless, butchered flesh. Instinctively, the simulacrum of Conan seemed to know that if he scattered the pieces far enough from each other, they would not be able to reunite. A kind of life would exist, but more akin to flora than fauna. To this end, the copy of a man kicked the scored sections of his attackers for a mile around the jungle. The fake Conan then returned to his assigned post, glowering at the jungle through fire-blue eyes.

The zombie Men With No Eyes had come to the end of their journey in a way they had never begun to expect.

Five thousand enthralled zombies stood gathered outside in the darkness. Neg stared at them from the ramparts of his castle. Half again enough to begin, he decided. And northwest seemed a good direction. He waved his left arm.

"Go. Kill all men in your path until you reach Numalia. Await there my pleasure."

Half of the force turned and shambled off in the darkness. What would the good folk of Numalia think when they saw an army of dead stop on their doorstep? What would they pay to be rid of them? Everything, eventually, but Neg would start by demanding wagons full of precious stones, gold, assorted virgins, and rare baubles as he decided upon at his leisure. Perhaps he would have a castle built of gold, with sidewalks of rubies and emeralds. An interesting idea.

The rest of the zombies he wished to keep close to home, for the moment. Any attacking force sent by those who might discern where the zombies originated would have to deal with his reserve, and they were formidable enough.

He turned away from the sight of the departing troops.

His conquest of the world had begun.

Had it been possible, Skeer would have been red with anger. As it stood, he showed no external sign of his rage, and that was just as well. Neg's power was such that should he become irritated, what he could or might do was unpredictable. Not that Skeer had done so well in predicting his master's behavior before he had grown so strong. Skeer the fool, Skeer the jester, Skeer the slackwit, to fall for such an old trick as poisoned wine. Why, he had used the same himself!

He walked through a lower portion of the castle, and the skitter of his dog spiders stayed the same as it had been since they had joined him. He had grown accustomed to it, especially since there was nothing to be done for it.

Ahead of him, he saw Tuanne walking his way.

"Ah. We meet again."

She did not speak, but continued walking, albeit slowly.

"Going to see our mutual master?"

"Aye," she said.

"Give him my regards: a pox upon him for a thousand years."

"Fallen out of favor, Skeer?"

He turned and began to walk next to her. "He calls you, eh? I would see your meeting, would he allow it."

"Can you think so badly of me, now that you suffer the same affliction?"

Skeer walked unspeaking for a few steps. Finally, he said, "Nay, I admit that I cannot. I can understand why you did what you did. Would that I could retrieve the talisman. I would put an end to this quickly enough."

"You know where it is?"

"Aye, for all the good it does. It is well guarded, and all of his enthralled are forbidden to even think of entering the saferoom."

"We are not forbidden such a thing," came Conan's voice from behind them.

Skeer spun. Tuanne twisted her neck to see, though she did not stop walking. "Conan!" she said. "And Elashi!"

"Aye. The salt, Elashi."

Skeer straightened from his crouch. "You have *salt*? Here?"

"Aye."

"Then cast it upon me, as well!"

Tuanne said, "It is ordinary salt, Skeer. It will not break his spell, it will only stop movement temporarily."

"Anything, so that I might resist his call. Please."

"I am not disposed to aid you, Skeer. You slew my friend."

"I can take you to the talisman," Skeer said. "You can stop Neg if you have that."

Conan looked at Tuanne.

"Yes," she said. "Please."

"Very well. Here is the water bottle, Elashi. Add your salt to it."

The woman complied, and in a moment, held a small amount of saline solution. She cupped her hand and poured the brine into it, then flung it at Tuanne. Tuanne stiffened, and Conan caught her before she fell. He laid her gently upon his cloak, upon the flagstones. "We shall return for you when this is done."

She could not speak, but he saw the sparkle in her eyes.

"And me?" Skeer said.

Conan looked down at the spiders, who seemed unperturbed at their presence. "After you show us where the talisman is held."

"Come, then, before Neg decides he needs his boots polished yet again, and calls for me."

With a last glance at Tuanne, Conan and Elashi followed Skeer, staying far enough back to avoid treading upon the spiders between them.

Twenty-one

"There are six guards," Skeer said. "Men With No Eyes. One of them is like I am, the others living."

"We shall deal with them," Conan said.

"First, we must reach them. Listen."

From around the bend in the corridor just ahead came the sound of voices approaching.

"Quickly, in there!" Skeer pointed at a nearby door. He led the way through it, with Elashi behind him and Conan following her.

Once inside the room—it was a storage area, with dozens of tapers hung by double strings and dark wooden barrels stacked two high along the walls—Conan left the door ajar a crack. He held his sword ready as he peered through the narrow opening.

Outside, half a dozen men moved past the impromptu hiding place. They all had that pale, wan look of the reawakened dead.

Next to him, Skeer said, "Neg has allowed many of the assembled throng inside, as a security measure. The halls are likely to be full of his new slaves."

"Then we shall have to be careful," Conan said.

"Could we not pass for more of the same?" Elashi asked.

"Nay. We recognize our own," Skeer replied.

"Perhaps we could pretend to be your prisoners," Conan said.

"Yes, that might work. Although I am no more than a lackey to Neg, many of the newly enzombied ones know I am at least a close lackey."

"Then let us proceed," the Cimmerian said.

Something was amiss, Neg felt. What, he could not say, but it was as if some worrisome itch troubled him, in a place he could not quite reach. There could be no need for alarm, not with the thousands of loyal nightwalkers gathered outside, along with the dozens of new ones within. He was invulnerable to ordinary attack, and he could draw not only upon the physical strength of his followers, but upon their stored minds, as well. What they knew he could know; he merely had to seek the answer.

What was it?

Hmm.

Well, for one thing, Tuanne was overdue to arrive. Perhaps he should check upon her progress.

He sent his mind searching for hers. Ah, there it was, quite close by. *Give me your eyes,* he commanded.

What he then saw made no sense. It seemed to be a blank wall, dimly lit, and practically featureless. After a moment he realized that it was not a wall, but a ceiling.

How could this be? Was she standing still and staring at a ceiling? That was impossible, since he had commanded her to attend him here. She might move slowly, but move she must.

Close your eyes, he said mentally.

Nothing happened. The ceiling stayed where it was.

Now that he observed it more closely, he could see that the height of it was more than usual. Were it in his castle, as indeed it must be, then Tuanne must be squatting, or even lying upon her back. And unable—certainly not unwilling—to close her eyes. The only way that could happen would be if she were under some sort of counterspell. A spell laid by another, more powerful wizard, or witch, perhaps? Or maybe just something as simple as a paralyzing solution of salt, none of which was allowed in the castle, save what Neg personally controlled.

Whatever the cause, it boded ill. This was a fly in the ointment, and it must be dealt with, immediately.

He broke his contact with Tuanne. Where was Skeer?

Never mind. He was of no importance. He clapped his hands, and two of his priests, still living (he would have to attend to that soon too), appeared. "Go and find Tuanne. Bring her here."

The priests bowed, and hurried out.

Still, the invisible itch persisted. Something more. And where had Skeer gotten to? Perhaps he should see what the ex-thief was up to . . . ?

Later, he decided.

The Disguise Master walked in tandem with Brute. They had been among the lucky ones admitted to the inner sanctum of Neg's castle. Brute now had his arm back. That had been interesting, watching the arm drag itself along by finger and wrist action, seeking its owner as might a crippled dog. Brute had bent and picked it up, then simply stuck it back where it belonged. It had healed within a matter of hours.

As had the cut in the Disguise Master's own head. Sealed over like a puddle of water in a winter storm. To all appearances, he looked no different than when he was alive. True, some of the zombies looked far worse than did he. Some wounds took much longer to heal, and where large portions of flesh or bone were missing, total repair did not occur. It made for some interesting scarring, and unbelievable locomotion, people stumping around on bare bones, in some cases.

Ah, well. It was not his to reason how or why. Even though he was in thrall to the necromancer, he had a kind of freedom. Better walking dead than rotting in the ground dead.

Tuanne lay on Conan's cloak, a prisoner within her own salt-frozen body. Neg had touched her mind, and had seen that she lay unmoving. Little doubt he would wonder about that, and no doubt that he would do something about it. Her only hope lay with Conan and Elashi.

As the dawn rose, a caravan of *notarii* performers journeying southward toward Koth began to break camp. One of the men striking his tent happened to glance at the next ridge over. He gasped, and quickly made the sign against evil in the chilly morning air before he began yelling the alert. "Zhombeya! Zhombeya!" he screamed.

The camp responded quickly. As the thousands of silent figures walked and slid down the face of the ridge, anything that could not be packed and carried rapidly was left behind. Before the approaching horde reached the site, the campers were long gone, moving at historically proper right angles to the zombies' march.

The *notarii* knew how to deal with Zhombeya, and the way of it was simple: Run. And run fast.

In their return from the dead, Neg's minions had apparently gained no more perception than they had when alive. As Conan and his two companions passed the third group of zombies, led by Skeer, they did so for the third time without questions. Either the patrolling groups thought Skeer in control, or they did not care. While Skeer had nodded at one death-brother he seemed to know, he had not needed to speak his prepared remarks:

"These are my prisoners. I am taking them to Neg."

That was what he was ready to state, but as yet, no one had seemed particularly interested in them.

These perverted creatures were not very observant. Conan still wore his sword, as did Elashi. This was going to be easier than Conan had thought.

"Conan!" came the yell that destroyed Conan's smugness.

He turned, to see the Disguise Master and Brute, both none the less for his having slain them.

"Best we move, fast!" Conan said.

The three of them broke into a run, away from the Disguise Master.

"After them! They are Neg's enemies!"

Those words were apparently the correct ones, for the dozen or so zombies in the hall began to chase them.

Conan drew his sword, but did not slow his pace. His pursuers were already dead, and while he could cut them down, he could not hope to disable a dozen of them quickly enough to win the victory. A wise man, his father had told him, knew when to run and when to fight. It was time to run.

They pounded around another bend in the corridor, to face another group of ten of the walking dead. Conan would have slashed a path through them, but Elashi's wit was quicker than his blade.

"Behind us!" she called. "Neg's enemies pursue us!"

"Neg's enemies" was definitely a triggering phrase. The ten were galvanized into action. They leaped to defend their master, no doubt mindlessly obeying his injunction to do just that, at any cost.

Conan, Elashi, and Skeer kept running, leaving the two groups to sort it out. Doubtless they would in short order, but Conan had no plans to stay and find out.

Enemies in his castle! How they had come to be there he could determine later; meanwhile, they had to be captured or destroyed!

Neg tugged at his mustache, twirling one end in nervousness. He would fill the castle with his enthralled; there would be no place for an enemy to hide!

He sent the call.

In a few moments, five hundred more of his nightwalkers would stalk the halls!

Skeer, trailing spiders, led Conan and Elashi down a flight of steep stone stairs. There were fewer of his creatures dogging him now, since Conan's large feet had flattened several in their flight, but those that remained stuck grimly and gamely on their path.

Behind them, pursuit thundered along the flagstones. No one came down the stairs, however.

Skeer said, "This way leads to the dungeon."

"What of the talisman?" Conan asked.

"Halfway around the castle. But we can cover a great part of the way by going under it."

"Lead on, then."

The last of Skeer's spiders, perhaps sixteen or eighteen of them, moved to one side, keeping well clear of Conan's footsteps.

Neg faced the one who called himself the Disguise Master. "Speak," he said.

"He is called 'Conan,' lord. An outland barbarian. He was the one who . . . slew me. He travels with a woman, though there was another woman with them earlier, a zombie—"

"What? Describe this zombie woman!"

The Disguise Master did.

Tuanne! Ah!

"We had scores to settle—"

"I am not interested in your petty arguments. Tell me more about this barbarian and woman."

"There was a third one with them, one of your enthralled."

"Really? Describe this one!"

"He has a face that would grace a sainted holy man. And a collection of spiders follows him—"

"Skeer! By Set's Black Coils! I shall grind his bones into powder! No, that would be too good for him. I shall have him rendered armless and legless and used as a footstool!"

Lost completely in a maze of hallways they were, and suddenly Skeer stopped. "Oh, no! He calls me."

If such a thing was possible, Skeer turned even whiter than he already was.

"He—he *knows*!"

"The Disguise Master," Elashi said.

"Aye," Conan agreed. "Use the salt solution."

The desert woman unstoppered the liquid and sprayed it at Skeer. The zombie went rigid, and Conan caught his stiffened form and lowered him to the floor next to the wall.

The remaining spiders formed a semi-circle around Skeer.

"We are on our own," Conan said. "Let us go and find this guarded room."

Elashi nodded. "I shall follow you."

Tuanne had regained some movement by the time the two Men With No Eyes finished carrying her to Neg's inner sanctum. The necromancer wore a smile that might have graced a demon contemplating some particularly hellish deed.

"Ah, the lovely Tuanne! We have much to discuss, you and I."

The priests set the zombie woman onto her feet. She swayed slightly, but managed to remain standing. She was lost, and there seemed no point in hoping any longer.

"What is the intent of this lout of whom I have only recently learned, this Conan?"

Though she tried to hold back the words, Neg's gaze compelled her to speak. "He—he seeks your death."

"My death? Ha! Thousands have desired such and thousands have failed to achieve it. Most of them found for themselves that which they would wish for me."

"And yet, he is inside your castle, is he not?"

Neg frowned. "You have learned insolence. I cannot permit this." He waved, and pointed one finger at Tuanne.

Pain seared her, as if a hot needle had been thrust into

her tender breast. She gasped, bent, then managed to straighten.

"Is this all this man wishes?"

She could not lie, she knew, but perhaps she could shade the truth. Conan no doubt wished many things, and certainly she did not know them all.

"I do not know all that he wishes." That was the truth; she had not lied to him—he had not asked *what* else Conan had planned. If he asked, she would have to tell him, but without that compulsion she had some small amount of control.

The necromancer tugged at his mustache. He twirled it and smiled. "No matter," he said. "Within a few moments the entire castle will swarm with my nightwalkers. Your hero will be captured and brought here for my amusement. Perhaps the two of you can perform certain . . . dances together for me."

Tuanne stood silently. Perhaps he was through with her for now. Hope stirred slightly, a nearly extinct hope, but not extinguished totally. Conan and Elashi were resourceful. Perhaps there was some small chance yet left.

"Is this Conan alone?"

The word came hard, but it came. "No."

"Ah. Who is with him?"

"Elashi, a woman of the desert."

"Ah." The demonic smile replayed. "The more the merrier. And would she have me dead, as well?"

"Yes."

He shook his head. "Yet another fool to join my army. Ah, well, with two women and one barbarian, I am sure I can devise some entertainment that will amuse me for a few moments."

Tuanne said nothing, but the small hope she held wavered. Neg was too powerful now, she could feel the energies radiate from him like heat from a bonfire. With a wave of his hand he could slay both Conan and Elashi, with no more effort than swatting a bothersome insect. Their only chance lay in finding the Source of Light and disrupting the power Neg now enjoyed.

At best, the odds were overwhelming.

Twenty-two

Conan began to feel like a butcher. He and Elashi had given up all pretense of secrecy. They ran along the corridors of the massive castle, twisting and turning, using their blades to clear a path when needed. The zombies could not die of sharp steel, but a sufficiently skilled and powerful stroke would slow them considerably. A man hopping on one leg moved much slower than the desert woman and Cimmerian. And heads were also good. A body without a head could not see to follow, until it had fetched that lopped off extremity, and that took time.

They ran, until finally they found by accident that which they sought. Six robed figures stood arrayed along the corridor with a door behind them. This must be the place, Conan thought.

The unarmed priests launched themselves at the two interlopers. They were fast, the Men With No Eyes, but the corridor was narrow enough so that they could not easily encircle Conan and Elashi.

Conan wove a deadly tapestry with his blade, cold blue iron dancing through warm flesh. He cut and slashed, leaped and pivoted, and quickly downed two of the attackers.

Elashi, behind him, kept one of the priests at bay with her blade, scoring on him with mostly shallow cuts, but enough to hold him at bay.

The remaining three danced and dodged, and kept Conan hopping to avoid being caught. He had the sword and great strength, but they were faster. And, he recalled, one of them was already dead. He had to take care not to allow that one—which was he?—to grasp his blade and pinion it while the others moved on him.

A snap kick caught Conan in the ribs on the left side. He grunted and chopped downward with his weapon. The sword bit into a thigh, but no blood welled. Ah, the zombie!

The undead priest snatched at the bloody blade, but Conan jerked it back, slicing off two of the zombie's fingers in the process. He wouldn't lose track of that one, at least.

Another of the blind men spun in, his right arm extended, fist doubled tightly. The whirling strike, aimed at Conan's temple, bounced, instead, off the muscular shoulder the Cimmerian hunched up at the final instant. Even though the meat of Conan's arm was both thick and hard, he felt the power of the punch vibrate him deeply.

Behind him, Elashi yelled, "Conan! Down the corridor!"

Conan lunged at the spinning priest and lanced the man's belly open with a surgical stab. As the priest fell, blocking his brothers for a moment, Conan took the time to look at Elashi's concern.

Crom! More of the undead shambled toward them. They had only a few seconds before they would be buried in attackers.

"The door!" Conan yelled.

He bounded over the fallen priest, slashed at the blind zombie, severing a hand, then turned toward the door.

Locked, of course.

Elashi managed to skewer her man. She jumped to aid Conan against the final pair.

The approaching zombie horde neared.

Conan leaped across the corridor, buried his sword in the gut of the living priest with a backhand slash, then threw his body against the locked door.

The mechanism of the lock had never been intended to withstand the weight of a Cimmerian giant at full force. The metal screeched and surrendered, and the door slammed open, Conan flying through the doorway. Elashi slipped in behind him. Before the nearest zombie could reach the entrance, Conan slammed the door shut and braced his hands against it.

"There it is!" Elashi said.

The muscles in Conan's arms and shoulders rippled as the zombies outside pounded and shoved against the door. "Well, fetch it!" he said, leaning against the wood. It moved open half an inch, then held. "And hurry!"

Conan looked over his shoulder as Elashi ran to the crystal stand. She hesitated, her hand over the talisman.

"It glows," she said.

"I care not if it sings and dances! Collect it!"

She snatched the talisman up. "I have it."

"Good. Stand next to the door. On this side."

She moved to obey.

"Stand ready," he ordered. With that, Conan leaped away from the door and in front of Elashi.

The door burst open and four zombies fell into the room. Conan grabbed Elashi and jumped over the sprawled bodies into the corridor.

Perhaps fifty of the undead had gathered there.

Well. He would meet Crom with arms sore from swinging a sword, Conan thought. He raised his blade.

Elashi said, "Wait!"

He looked at her. She held the talisman—it was glowing, a kind of greenish light coming from it—out in front of her.

The zombies backed away from her, as though in fear.

Quickly, she jumped forward and touched one of them with the talisman. He fell, and as he did, shriveled as a leaf dropped into fire.

"She bears the True Death!" somebody said.

At this, half of the zombies turned and ran. The others moved toward Conan and Elashi, but no longer threatening. They smiled.

"Me," one said, "touch me first!"

"And then me," another said. "Bless you!"

Conan was puzzled for a moment.

"They wish to die," Elashi said quietly. "The talisman's touch will free them to return to the Gray Lands."

Conan nodded. "Touch them. Then let us find Neg and touch him—with this." Conan shook his sword.

A small village in the middle of nowhere waited for destruction. They had heard of the zombie march, of the thousands who killed all before them, and those who had not fled knew there was no hope.

But, as the killers approached, a strange thing happened: they stopped. They moved not, but simply stood and stared, as if seeing something a thousand miles away.

It was, the villagers later said, as if they had run out of intent.

Neg's anger filled the room.

"The talisman! It has been moved! My power wanes!"

Still in thrall, Tuanne managed a smile. He controlled

her, and many of the others in the castle, but outside of that, the magic that fueled Neg's power would fall off dramatically.

The necromancer spun and faced Tuanne. "You! Your barbarian did this!"

"I hope so," she said.

"Bitch! You will twist for this!" He stabbed a finger at her, but Tuanne felt no stabbing fire this time. Her smile continued unabated.

"I shall deal with you later!" He turned and stalked from the room.

The solution of saltwater Elashi had used upon him must have either been weak or in insufficient quantity, Skeer realized. Movement returned to his limbs much sooner than he would have thought. He stood, and the ever-present spiders scuttled back a little. He sighed. Neg's punishment for his transgressions would be most unpleasant, of that he was certain. But—wait—the compulsion was gone! What had happened? He felt for the undeniable command, but Neg must be occupied elsewhere, for he could not sense any presence. Odd.

Skeer had never been one to look a gift's origins over too closely. He had to get to the talisman.

Conan and Elashi moved down the corridor, and left bodies piled upon the floor as they walked. Many of the undead came to embrace the Source of Light, though now the Cimmerian thought it more the Source of Death. Others still fled when they felt the power. Conan wondered if a direct touch was needed. He suspected it was not, but he had no notion of how to operate the device, and it was just as well. That kind of power could be seductive. Better a man did not tempt himself that way.

They moved down the hall, the only two living people, re-releasing to death the souls of all who wished it.

Neg stormed along the corridors, rage stirring his black heart. He would find this barbarian and he would turn his death-gaze upon the fool until the man withered into ash! The disruption in his plans did more than irritate him, it was an affront to his entire being! He had not lived all the centuries, planning and scheming to get this far to be stopped by some *barbarian*!

Skeer, spiders in tow, reached Neg's crystal chamber. The bodies lying sprawled were so deeply piled in places he had to climb over them, to see that the room no longer held the magical device. So. Conan and the woman had managed to beat Neg's formidable defenses. Amazing.

He began to follow the trail of corpses, some of which now were little more than dry bones. When the True Death claimed them, the preserving spell had vanished, and the corruption had been vastly accelerated. Or, perhaps, maybe just resumed where it had left off before Neg's call. That thought pleasured him not at all, especially when he contemplated his own dissolution; still, if somehow Neg lost control of him permanently, then he could adjust to living—or not living—this way. Something could be found to replace women and hemp. What, he could not say, but with enough time, something could be arranged.

The trick, then, was to see that Neg died or was rendered permanently inert somehow, without losing his own semblance of life. Might be tricky, that.

He hurried along, searching for Conan and Elashi.

The spiders crawled over the bodies, apparently without the slightest bit of interest in them.

*   *   *

Once-bright tapestries hung on the walls of the central meeting chamber, a room large enough to seat a hundred comfortably. The years had faded the drapes to dull tones, and layers of dust and cobwebs coated the long table down the center of the room. The skylight allowed the rays of the morning sun into the chamber, albeit filtered through iron bars thick with red rust. The nearly perpetual rain had yet to make its appearance on this morn, and the chamber held enough light to see with clarity.

Into the central room came Neg, through the south hallway.

At the same moment, Conan and Elashi entered the chamber via the north corridor.

Slightly behind Conan, Skeer and his tarantulas moved.

The four stood still for a heartbeat.

"So," Neg said. "*You* are the cause of my consternation!"

"Aye," Conan said, hefting his sword. "And you caused the death of my friend."

"I have caused many deaths, barbarian. I deal in death."

"My father among them," Elashi said.

Neg laughed. "And you, Skeer? Have you a complaint?"

Skeer hesitated. If Neg triumphed . . .

"No matter," Neg said. "Your treachery has earned you my ire. When these two fall, I shall attend to you."

Skeer felt his stomach roil.

Conan shifted his feet into a fighting stance, sword raised. He began to inch forward in small, carefully balanced steps.

Neg stood with his arms folded, watching.

Elashi raised her sword and also moved for Neg.

The necromancer affected a pose of disdain.

Conan saw that the man bore no weapons, at least none that were obvious. Ordinarily, he would care little for striking down an unarmed man, but Neg hardly fit into the category of ordinary. A quick, clean death was too good for him, but it was Conan's way; he would not stoop to torture.

When the Cimmerian was nearly close enough to leap and destroy the wizard, Neg raised one hand and held stiffened fingers pointing at Conan. "My eyes," he said.

Without thinking, Conan glanced up to lock gazes with the other man.

And could not look away.

Neg's eyes seemed to swirl with color, and they bored into Conan like a dagger. Suddenly, Conan felt his knees grow weak, as did his arms. The sword drooped, and he felt as if he were moving through thick mud. . . .

Elashi darted in then, her shorter blade raised to split Neg's skull. He snapped his gaze from Conan to the woman. She stopped, as if running into a rubbery wall. The sword fell from her fingers, and she sat down and covered her eyes with her hands, sobbing.

Conan felt some of his strength return, and he gathered himself to spring at the necromancer.

Neg looked away from Elashi and back at the Cimmerian, and the weakness enveloped him like a weighted blanket. Lifting the anvil at the trader's seemed easy compared to keeping his eyes open. If he could just lie down and rest for a moment, he could slay the villain later. . . .

"Do not sleep!" Skeer yelled. "It is the death-gaze! You will never awake if you stop now!"

Neg smiled at Skeer. "I have had enough of your crossings, Skeer!"

With that, Neg waved both hands in Skeer's direction, as if casting dust.

Conan managed to look at Skeer. The zombie groaned, and began to shrivel. In a few seconds, he looked like a grape left in the sun too long. The moan caught in his throat, and he fell. His skin turned to parchment, his flesh seemed to melt from under it, and after three heartbeats, a mummified skeleton lay on the chamber floor where Skeer had been.

The big spiders swarmed over the corpse, highly agitated.

"Now," Neg said, "to finish this unpleasant business."

He turned back toward Conan.

Conan struggled to take the final two steps that would allow him to reach Neg. He managed one, and then stopped, as if cast in iron. He could not move. He could hear Elashi crying softly behind him, and he regretted that she would die, but there was nothing he could do. He would not give up, but he could . . . not . . . move. . . .

Neg screamed.

Conan shook his head as the spell slackened slightly.

It was the spiders. They attacked Neg. He slapped at them, smashing and flinging them from him, but those who were not killed darted back at him, clambering up his legs and biting wherever they could reach.

With the fall of Skeer, the spiders' confusion ended. Skeer was dead, but his essence was finally seen to have been transferred to Neg. And Neg was alive. They could now fulfill their mission, the Shes, and so they did.

Conan raised the sword. It weighed as much as a boulder! He shuffled his foot forward half an inch. His feet were nailed to the floor—

"Die!" Neg screamed.

The spiders fell away from him, rolling onto their backs, some of them, legs fluttering in the still air.

Conan strained against a mountain in his way, shoving as though through solid rock—

Neg looked up from the twitching spiders at Conan.

"No!" He shot one hand up—

Conan contracted the muscles of his back and shoulders and stomach and brought the sword down with all the power he had left—

The edge of the sharped blue iron hit Neg square on the head. The *chunk!* of the blade opening the skull was lost in a sudden rush of what seemed a foul wind bursting forth from Neg's head. The stench gagged Conan, and he released the sword and fell to his knees.

The tapestries blew in the unnatural wind. The dust in the chamber stirred into a blinding storm. Conan rubbed at his eyes.

When it cleared, on the floor next to Conan was a pool of corruption, a greasy puddle of red and black fluid, oozing over the flagstones.

And Neg the Malefic was no more.

Twenty-three

At a village in the middle of nowhere, a great cry suddenly rent the air as the voices of many dead-undead thousands gave out a ragged cheer.

Partial freedom had been achieved.

In Neg's inner sanctum, Conan and Elashi found Tuanne, freed of the necromancer's control. The two women wept for joy, and Conan had to admit to himself that he was happy to see the zombie girl, not to mention being more than a little pleased at still being alive.

"You killed him," Tuanne said.

"Conan did," Elashi said. "With the help of Skeer's spiders, of all things." She explained the final battle with Neg.

When she had done, Tuanne smiled. "A brave man, is our Conan." Both women turned to smile at him.

"And now what?" Conan said, feeling suddenly uncomfortable somehow.

"We must use the talisman to free the walking dead," Tuanne said. "If you will help me? I cannot touch the Source directly."

229

'Of course,'' Elashi said.

The two women drew aside. Conan heard them mumbling together. He kept one portion of his mind on the women, but another part stayed alert for any of the zombies or Men With No Eyes who might still be lurking about the castle. Correction, the *stinking* castle: the odor that permeated the air made the smell of a charnel house seem like delicate flowers. Breathing such noxious fumes could hardly be a healthy, worthwhile endeavor.

"Best we go outside," Tuanne said.

"Aye."

The three of them went to the lowered drawbridge and crossed the moat. Once outside, they turned back to face the castle. If anything living—or dead—stirred save themselves, Conan could not see it.

"Hold the device thusly," Tuanne said. She gestured, and Elashi took the proper grip from her example.

"Yes. Now, say the words, Quodnecesant—"

Elashi repeated the words.

"—sibidamnononerit—"

"—sibidamnononerit—" Elashi finished.

There came a rumble from within the castle. The sky over it suddenly seemed to brighten. No, it *did* grow brighter! Almost as if a new sun had appeared there—

Conan blinked against the glare.

The light flashed, then, sending out thousands of beams, like a stylized rendition of the sun done by a mad artist. As quickly as it had come, the glow died.

The Disguise Master, running tirelessly next to Brute, with whom he now had much more in common than before, saw the man next to him speared with a lance of bright light. A second later, he felt a similar spear enter his own spine.

Both died the True Death instantly.

Malo the priest rejoined his ancestors in the Gray Lands, transfixed by the fiery rod for a second before he tumbled from a high mountain pass into eternity.

All over the land, those who had been plucked from the afterlife by Neg's sorcery were returned to it. Outside the nameless village, several thousand fell at once, as if they were puppets with their strings cut by a giant razor.

Totally free now, they were.

And outside the castle Tuanne turned to Elashi. "If you would wrap the talisman in a piece of cloth or purse, please?"

Elashi dropped the Source of Light into her purse, pulled the leather bag from her belt, and passed it to Tuanne.

"Thank you. My proximity to it, oddly enough, protected me from the splash that took my fellow zombies." She hefted the bag. "I will touch it directly. There are some nice trees over there, I think I shall do it there."

Elashi started to cry. "Must you? I—we have come to care for you." She glanced at Conan, who nodded briefly.

"Come here," Tuanne said softly.

When Conan and Elashi were close enough, Tuanne put her arms around both of them, and hugged them tightly. "You have been lovers and friends to me," she said, "and I shall remember you through all eternity. But I must go. I am a hundred years past my time."

Elashi's tears continued to stream.

Conan turned his head away for a moment, to brush at something that had gotten into his eye.

Elashi said, "W-w-would you like us to . . . to—?"

"No. I would rather you remember me as I am now," Tuanne said. "It will be quick, and there will be little left, after a hundred years."

Conan rubbed at his other eye. Dust, it had to be.

"Fare thee well," Tuanne said. She turned, and walked toward a small grove of evergreen trees. Elashi watched her go, until Conan tugged gently at her arm.

"What are you doing?"

"She wants privacy," Conan said. "Let us give her that."

Elashi turned toward Conan and pressed her face against his chest.

"Do you still wish the talisman? I could retrieve it for you, after Tuanne—"

"No. Let it rest with her bones. Better that we should both remember her as she was."

"Aye."

They walked away from the edge of the moat, and Conan felt a discomfort he could not quite define.

"What will you do now?" Conan asked.

"Return to my tribe in the desert," Elashi said. "I must report upon this to my brothers and uncles. And what of you?" Elashi asked.

Conan shrugged. "I was bound for Zamora before. I see no reason to change my destination."

"Shall we travel together until I turn south? I suddenly feel alone."

"Aye," Conan said. "Why not?"

The two of them walked away from the dead castle, and neither looked back at the small grove of evergreen trees.

A Conan Chronology
by
Robert Jordan

Over the years during which I wrote novels about Conan
of Cimmeria, I frequently received letters from fans
inquiring about the proper placement in Conan's life of
the various novels (both mine and those by other au-
thors), and even of the short stories and novellas. Several of the true Conan aficionados even sent me copies
of chronologies they had themselves worked out for all
of the then-published works. It was seldom that two of
these agreed in every detail with either each other or
with the order in which I believe the stories belong.
Sometimes they diverged widely.

Now that I am editing the novels rather than writing
them, I receive fewer of these queries and chronologies,
but they still come in occasionally. As an aid to those
real Conan fans, I present this chronology of all of the
Conan stories and novels published to this time.

This chronology is primarily a simple listing of the
stories in the order in which they occur in the life of
the Cimmerian, which I originally prepared after I stopped

writing Conan novels for distribution to other writers who wanted to take up Robert E. Howard's mantle. In a few cases, where there are questions about the exact placement of a story, a note will give the alternate placement. There are a number of notes at the end of the list, most of which refer to the early publishing history of the original Robert E. Howard stories. Some of the notes give the facts about stories which L. Sprague de Camp (in some cases with assistance from Lin Carter or Bjorn Nyberg) finished, rewrote, and/or edited from outlines or rough drafts prepared by Howard. In instances where a story has appeared under more than one name, I have attempted to list these alternative names as well. It is possible that I have missed a variation somewhere, but I have tried to be as thorough as I could. The note which applies to a particular story will be designated by a number (as #1, #2, etc.) after the name of the author.

I am well aware in undertaking this that there will be disagreements among the readers over whether I have put every story in its proper place. That is all well and good. If you disagree, let me know about it. Perhaps you will even convince me.

TITLE	AUTHOR
"Legions of the Dead"	de Camp/Carter
"The Thing in the Crypt"	de Camp/Carter
CONAN THE DEFIANT	Perry
"The Tower of the Elephant"	HOWARD #1
CONAN THE RAIDER	Carpenter
CONAN AND THE SORCERER	Offutt #2

CONAN THE MERCENARY	Offutt #2
CONAN: THE SWORD OF SKELOS	Offutt #2
CONAN THE DESTROYER	Jordan #3
CONAN THE MAGNIFICENT	Jordan
CONAN THE INVINCIBLE	Jordan
"The Hall of the Dead"	HOWARD/de Camp #4
CONAN THE FEARLESS	Perry
"The God in the Bowl"	HOWARD #5
"Rogues in the House"	HOWARD #6
CONAN THE VICTORIOUS	Jordan
CONAN THE CHAMPION	Roberts #7
CONAN THE UNCONQUERED	Jordan
"The Hand of Nergal"	HOWARD/Carter
"The People of the Summit"	de Camp/Nyberg
"The City of Skulls"	de Camp/Carter
"The Curse of the Monolith"	de Camp/Carter #8
CONAN AND THE SPIDER GOD	de Camp
"The Bloodstained God"	HOWARD/de Camp #9
CONAN THE VALOROUS	Roberts
"The Frost Giant's Daughter"	HOWARD #10
"The Lair of the Ice Worm"	de Camp/Carter
CONAN THE DEFENDER	Jordan

CONAN: THE ROAD OF KINGS	Wagner #11
CONAN THE TRIUMPHANT	Jordan
"Queen of the Black Coast"	HOWARD #12
CONAN THE REBEL	Anderson #13
"The Vale of Lost Women"	HOWARD #14
"The Castle of Terror"	de Camp/Carter
"The Snout in the Dark"	HOWARD/de Camp/ Carter #15
"Hawks Over Shem"	HOWARD/de Camp #16
"Black Colossus"	HOWARD #17
"Shadows in the Dark"	de Camp/Carter
CONAN THE RENEGADE	Carpenter
"Shadows in the Moonlight"	HOWARD #18
"The Road of the Eagles"	HOWARD/de Camp #19
"A Witch Shall Be Born"	HOWARD #20
"Black Tears"	de Camp/Carter
"Shadows in Zamboula"	HOWARD #21
"The Star of Khorala"	de Camp/Nyberg
"The Devil in Iron"	HOWARD #22
"The Flame Knife"	HOWARD/de Camp #23 (novella)
"The People of the Black Circle"	HOWARD #24 (novella)
"The Slithering Shadow"	HOWARD #25
"Drums of Tombalku"	HOWARD/de Camp #26
"The Gem in the Tower"	de Camp/Carter
"The Pool of the Black One"	HOWARD #27

CONAN THE BUCCANEER	de Camp/Carter
"Red Nails"	HOWARD #28 (novella)
"Jewels of Gwahlur"	HOWARD #29
"The Ivory Goddess"	de Camp/Carter
"Beyond the Black River"	HOWARD #30
"Moon of Blood"	de Camp/Carter
"The Treasure of Tranicos"	HOWARD/de Camp #31 (novella)
"Wolves Beyond the Border"	HOWARD/de Camp #32 De Camp/Carter
CONAN THE LIBERATOR	
"The Phoenix on the Sword"	HOWARD #33
"The Scarlet Citadel"	HOWARD #34
CONAN THE CONQUEROR	HOWARD #35
THE RETURN OF CONAN	de Camp/Nyberg #36
"The Witch of the Mists"	de Camp/Carter
"Black Sphinx of Nebthu"	de Camp/Carter
"Red Moon of Zembabwei"	de Camp/Carter
"Shadows in the Skull"	de Camp/Carter
CONAN OF THE ISLES	de Camp/Carter

NOTES

#1. "The Tower of the Elephant" was first published in *Weird Tales* for March 1933. It was reprinted in *SKULL-FACE AND OTHERS* (ROBERT E. HOWARD), Arkham House, 1946; and in *THE COMING OF CONAN* (ROBERT E. HOWARD), Gnome Press, 1953.

#2. *CONAN AND THE SORCERER, CONAN THE MERCENARY*, and *CONAN: THE SWORD OF SKELIOS* (all Andrew J. Offutt) may all three (in the same order) properly come later, after "Rogues in the House." The placement above is based on Conan's stated age of seventeen, but, as L. Sprague de Camp points out, he behaves in a much more sophisticated fashion than he properly should at that age. It should be noted that the three are linked together in such a fashion as to be able to be read as one novel, though they stand well alone.

#3. *CONAN THE DESTROYER* (Robert Jordan), the novelization of the movie of the same name may properly be placed later, after "Rogues in the House." L. Sprague de Camp places it *before* the three novels by Andrew J. Offutt.

#4. "The Hall of the Dead" was first published in *The Magazine of Science Fiction and Fantasy* for February 1967. It was written by L. Sprague de Camp to an outline found by Glenn Lord among Robert Howard's papers in 1966.

#5. "The God in the Bowl" was first published in *Space Science Fiction* for September 1952. It was reprinted in *THE COMING OF CONAN* (ROBERT E. HOWARD), Gnome Press, 1953.

#6. "Rogues in the House" was first published in *Weird Tales* for January 1934. It was reprinted in *TERROR BY NIGHT* (ed. Christine Campbell Thomson), Selwyn & Blount, Ltd., 1934; in *SKULL-FACE AND OTHERS* (ROBERT E. HOWARD), Arkham House, 1946; in *THE COMING OF CONAN* (ROBERT

E. HOWARD), Gnome Press, 1953; and in *MORE NOT AT NIGHT* (ed. Christine Campbell Thomson), Arrow Books Ltd., 1961.

#7. *CONAN THE CHAMPION* (John Maddox Roberts) may properly be placed later, after "Shadows in the Moonlight" and before "The Road of Eagles."

#8. "The Curse of the Monolith" was originally published in *Worlds of Fantasy*, Vol. 1, No. 1, 1968, as "Conan and the Cenotaph."

#9. "The Bloodstained God" was rewritten by L. Sprague de Camp from a Robert Howard story, "The Trail of the Blood-Stained God," set in contemporary (1930s) Afghanistan. It was first published in *TALES OF CONAN* (ROBERT E. HOWARD/L. Sprague de Camp), Gnome Press, 1955.

#10. "The Frost Giant's Daughter" was first published under the title "Gods of the North" in *The Fantasy Fan* for March 1934, and was reprinted in *Fantastic Universe Science Fiction* for December 1956. In a version that had been revised by Robert Howard, and which was later revised again by L. Sprague de Camp, it was reprinted in *Fantasy Fiction* for August 1953 and in *THE COMING OF CONAN* (ROBERT E. HOWARD), Gnome Press, 1953, under its present title.

#11. *CONAN: THE ROAD OF KINGS* (Karl Edward Wagner) possibly belongs later, after "Hawks Over Shem" and before "Black Colossus."

#12. "Queen of the Black Coast" was first published in *Weird Tales* for May 1934. It was reprinted in

AVON FANTASY READER No. 8, 1948, and again in
THE COMING OF CONAN (ROBERT E. HOWARD),
Gnome Press, 1953.

#13. The occurrences of *CONAN THE REBEL* (Poul
Anderson) are generally considered to have taken place
between the events of Chapters 1 and 2 of "Queen of
the Black Coast."

#14. "The Vale of Lost Women" was first published
in *Magazine of Horror, No. 15*, Spring, 1967.

#15. "The Snout in the Dark" was rewritten by L.
Sprague de Camp and Lin Carter from an outline and
the first half of a rough draft of the story by Robert
Howard.

#16. "Hawks Over Shem" was rewritten by L. Sprague
de Camp from a Robert Howard story set in eleventh-
century Egypt and entitled "Hawks Over Egypt." It
was first published in *Fantastic Universe Science Fiction*
for October 1955. It was reprinted in *TALES OF CONAN*
(ROBERT E. HOWARD/L. Sprague de Camp), Gnome
Press, 1955.

#17. "Black Colossus" was first published in *Weird
Tales* for June 1933. It was reprinted in *CONAN THE
BARBARIAN*, Gnome Press, 1954. This should not be
confused with the movie novelization of the same name.
See Note #37.

#18. "Shadows in the Moonlight" was first published
in *Weird Tales* for April 1934. It was reprinted in
CONAN THE BARBARIAN, Gnome Press, 1954. This

should not be confused with the movie novelization of the same name. See Note #37.

#19. "The Road of the Eagles" was rewritten by L. Sprague de Camp from a story of the same name, by Robert Howard, set in the sixteenth-century Turkish Empire. Under the title "Conan, Man of Destiny," it was first published in *Fantastic Universe Science Fiction* for December 1955. It was reprinted in *TALES OF CONAN* (ROBERT E. HOWARD), Gnome Press, 1955, under its present title.

#20. "A Witch Shall Be Born" was first published in *Weird Tales* for December 1934. It was reprinted in *AVON FANTASY READER No. 10*, 1949; and in *CONAN THE BARBARIAN*, Gnome Press, 1954. This last should not be confused with the movie novelization of the same name. See Note #37.

#21. "Shadows in Zamboula" was first published in *Weird Tales* for November 1935. It was reprinted in *SKULL-FACE AND OTHERS* (ROBERT E. HOWARD), Arkham House, 1946; and in *CONAN THE BARBARIAN*, Gnome Press, 1954. This last should not be confused with the movie novelization of the same name. See Note #37.

#22. "The Devil in Iron" was first published in *Weird Tales* for August 1935. It was reprinted in CONAN *THE BARBARIAN*, Gnome House, 1954. This should not be confused with the movie novelization of the same name. See Note #37.

#23. "The Flame Knife" was first published in *TALES*

OF CONAN (ROBERT E. HOWARD), Gnome Press, 1955.

#24. "The People of the Black Circle" was first published, as a serial, in *Weird Tales* for September, October, and November 1934. It was reprinted in *THE SWORD OF CONAN* (ROBERT E. HOWARD), Gnome Press, 1952.

#25. "The Slithering Shadow" was first published in *Weird Tales* for September 1933. It was reprinted in *THE SWORD OF CONAN* (ROBERT E. HOWARD), Gnome Press, 1952.

#26. "Drums of Tombalku" was written/edited by L. Sprague de Camp from an outline and a partial rough draft found among Robert Howard's papers by Glenn Lord in 1965.

#27. "The Pool of the Black One" was first published in *Weird Tales* for October 1933. It was reprinted in *THE SWORD OF CONAN* (ROBERT E. HOWARD), Gnome Press, 1952.

#28. "Red Nails" was first published, as a serial, in *Weird Tales* for July, August-September, and October 1936. It was reprinted in *TALES OF CONAN* (ROBERT E. HOWARD), Gnome Press, 1952.

#29. "Jewels of Gwahlur" was first published in *Weird Tales* for March 1935. It was reprinted in *KING CONAN* (ROBERT E. HOWARD), Gnome Press, 1953.

#30. "Beyond the Black River" was first published in

Weird Tales for May and June 1935. It was reprinted in *KING CONAN* (ROBERT E. HOWARD), Gnome Press, 1953.

#31. "The Treasures of Tranicos" was first published, in an abridged form as revised by L. Sprague de Camp, as "The Black Stranger" in *Fantasy Magazine* for March 1953. It was first printed under the present title in *KING CONAN* (ROBERT E. HOWARD), Gnome Press, 1953.

#32. "Wolves Beyond the Border" was written/edited by L. Sprague de Camp from an outline and the first half of a story by Robert Howard, which were found by Glenn Lord among Robert Howard's papers in 1965. The events of this story occur simultaneously with *CONAN THE LIBERATOR*. This is the only story in the canon in which Conan does not appear.

#33. "The Phoenix on the Sword" was first published in *Weird Tales* for December 1932. It was reprinted in *SKULL-FACE AND OTHERS* (ROBERT E. HOWARD), Arkham House, 1946; and in *KING CONAN* (ROBERT E. HOWARD), Gnome Press, 1953.

#34. "The Scarlet Citadel" was first published in *Weird Tales* for January 1933. It was reprinted in *SKULL-FACE AND OTHERS* (ROBERT E. HOWARD), Arkham House, 1946; and in *KING CONAN* (ROBERT E. HOWARD), Gnome Press, 1953.

#35. *CONAN THE CONQUEROR* (ROBERT E. HOWARD) was originally serialized in *Weird Tales* for December 1935, January, February, March, and April 1936 under the title "The Hour of the Dragon." It is the only full-length novel about Conan written by Howard, though it was never published as a novel during his life.

#36. Chapters 2 through 5 of *THE RETURN OF CONAN* (L. Sprague de Camp/Bjorn Nyberg) were first published as a novella, "Conan the Victorious," in *Fantastic Universe Science Fiction* for September 1957. It was published under the listed title (with ten chapters, along with a prologue and an epilogue) by Gnome Press, 1957. The novella "Conan the Victorious" should not be confused with the later novel of the same name.

#37. *CONAN THE BARBARIAN* (L. Sprague & Catherine de Camp), the novelization of the movie of the same name, must be considered to lie outside the proper canon and chronology, though L. Sprague de Camp, in "Conan the Indestructible" (included in the Conan novels published by Tor Books) manages to fit it in as a variant early-life story. It is not to be confused with the collection of the same name published by Gnome Press in 1954.

LIST OF CONAN AUTHORS

Robert E. Howard was, of course, the creator of Conan
of Cimmeria and the Hyborian world, but since his
death a number of other writers have continued the tale
of Conan's life. These writers are listed here alphabet-
ically:

ROBERT E. HOWARD
Poul Anderson
Catherine de Camp
L. Sprague de Camp
Leonard Carpenter
Lin Carter
Roland Green (to be published)
Robert Jordan
Bjorn Nyberg
Andrew J. Offutt
Steve Perry
John Maddox Roberts
Karl Edward Wagner